Frederic S. Crofoot

Detroit Unveiled

Frederic S. Crofoot

Detroit Unveiled

ISBN/EAN: 9783744657228

Printed in Europe, USA, Canada, Australia, Japan

Cover: Foto ©Andreas Hilbeck / pixelio.de

More available books at **www.hansebooks.com**

DETROIT UNVEILED.

A GRAPHIC AND STARTLING REVELATION
OF THE MYSTERIES OF MICHIGAN'S
METROPOLIS.

BY

FREDERIC S. CROFOOT,

[Formerly Editor Detroit Sunday Sun.]

I have yet to learn that a lesson of the purest good may not be drawn from
the vilest evil. I have always believed this to be a recognized and established
truth, laid down by the best and wisest men the world has ever seen, constantly
acted upon by the best and wisest natures, and confirmed by the reason and
experience of every thinking mind.—CHARLES DICKENS.

HANDSOMELY ILLUSTRATED
BY W. A. HALL.

DETROIT:
SUNDAY WORLD PRINT.
1887.

A THIRD EDITION.

"Detroit Unveiled"

Has been received with such remarkable favor by the public that a third edition will be issued in about two weeks. The book will then contain several new and attractive features.

SINGING ITS PRAISES.

What the press generally and the Wayne County Courier in particular think of "Detroit Unveiled."

The following is a sample of the many favorable press notices of "Detroit Unveiled:"

"Detroit Unveiled," by Frederic S. Crofoot, is the latest addition to sensational literature. The author has been exploring the muddy by-paths and crooked lanes running through the dark side of Detroit's social world, and gives his curious experience in a terse, well written style. The book is illustrated with some well executed engravings and is neatly bound. It is sure to have a large sale.—WAYNE COUNTY COURIER.

AN EYE-OPENER.

The announcement of the publication of "Detroit Unveiled" has aroused the fiercest palpitations in the heart of the young and fragile slim, while the more antiquated article, he of the glistening pate and rubicund proboscis, has simply gasped in silent and inexplicable alarm; other gentlemen of sportive and festive natures have been teetering on the edge of a wild, weired and awful despair; but members of the criminal class have suffered the most. They have been simply palsied with fear.

It has been a staggerer!

"And how does it go?" was asked of a leading newsdealer.

"Like hot cakes!" came the reply, "nothing like it! even ministers are after it to catch new ideas for their sermons! I tell you its a corker!"

CONTENTS:

INTRODUCTION

I MAKE my bow.

Slow, graceful and courteous.

And with my most winning and attractive smile.

Like all authors who place their wares before the public I deem this form of obeisance necessary.

My book?

Pshaw! I will not trouble you here with a detailed discription of its contents. I would only tire you and myself as well.

INTRODUCTION.

Life is short and sweet, and brevity is the soul of wit.

The kernel of the nut is not worth the eating when it takes too long to get at it.

Suffice to say that the chapters deal with those persons and scenes in life which are not as a rule the subject of parlor gossip, but which by reading, nevertheless, cannot help but result in more good than harm.

However, if they be not discussed in the parlor they are often the fruitful and eloquent theme of the pulpit. I believe with those reverend and talented gentlemen, Mr. Talmage and the late lamented Mr. Beecher, and also Rev. Mr. Rexford, of Detroit, that the dregs of life will serve the purpose of a moral as well as its froth and cream.

But the book?

It deals with those flash scenes and incidents in real life, which cannot help but interest as well as instruct; putting the unwarry as well as wary on their guard; serving as a guide and protector to the young, innocent and unsophisticated; standing indeed, as a shining "pointer" to all who may be unacquainted with the sins, vices and crimes of a great city.

THE AUTHOR.

CHAPTER I.

The Ferry Boat Adventuress.

DURING the summer months the large and magnificent steamers on the Detroit river present a gala-like appearance with their gay colored bunting and flying flags. The bright dresses, ribbons and flowers of the fair lady passengers and the sweet melodious strains from Italian harps lend additional life and spirit to the scene.

In the eventide the river is indeed beautiful in appearance. The darting flames on the Western skies are mirrored in beautiful hues on the surface of the river. Then night creeps on apace with its sable mantle—a mantle rich and resplendant in a bead-work of twinkling stars.

The beauty, wealth and culture of Detroit seek the river for pleasure and diversion. There we find the calm and dignified man of business; the prim and stately matron with her merry-voiced, rosy-cheeked children; the dark-eyed coquette in all her witchery of glances and bonnet, doing her utmost to attract the attention of the handsome, blase gallant on the opposite side of the boat and hundreds of others, both male and female, from nearly every calling in life down to the bespangled, powdered, and yellow wigged woman of the town.

The river boats afford rare opportunities for flirting. We do not see the like in the ball-room, the theater or even on the street. There all restraint, reserve or prudery seems to fly away with the winds. Masculine advances are quickly received by smiles and handkerchief waving.

Affaires d'amour.

Ah me! Wicked sinful Detroit! They are without number.

What a beautiful woman! How shy—how modest—how retiring!

She sits with bowed head scanning the pages of one Ouida's latest novels. I notice the fine, keen, profile, as delicately chiseled as that of any Grecian maid; the long, dark lashes, the lily white complexion and the rosebud mouth. By her side is a young miss scarcely more than seven or eight.

But the fair creature reading the novel rivets my attention.

Do I find myself sighing? Pshaw! foolish fellow that I am!

I turn away and finally seek the lower deck. Leaning over the boat railing I thoughtfully puff away on my cigar. For awhile I find amusement in blowing the smoke into the air. But this soon grows tiresome. I find myself looking towards the stairway. I can resist no longer and again go to the deck above.

But I am greeted with a startling scene.

An elderly gentleman sits near my fair young lady and has engaged her in conversation. I watch them closely. The man is eager and impulsive, while she, sweet demure young thing! bends her blushing face still closer to her book, and save a few coy glances now and then, seems to be unheedful of his presence.

My lips close in a malicious, sardonic chuckle. I feel revenged!

Revenged! And why? Because now I know my beautiful charmer.

They leave the boat together. A coupe takes them to a private dining room. They drink champagne and eat only the delicacies of the season. He is rich and can easily afford it.

And both are willing.

In the evening they drive up to her home. She slyly places 'one tiny dimpled finger on his lips.

"Be careful! Don't attract the attention of the neighbors."

"But your husband!"

"There now, old goosey! Didn't I tell you he was in Chicago."

He hesitates. Not long however! The beautiful figure and face are too much for him. Unconsciously he finds himself muttering:

"Damn her husband!"

"What's that you say?" demurely.

"Oh, nothing! Only thinking what a beautiful woman you are!"

"There you are again! Won't you ever stop?"

"Never!" responded her enamoured companion, with decided emphasis.

They look into each other's face and smile.

The little child in the meantime is soundly sleeping. She is awakened and the three pass into the house.

The gentleman is seated in the parlor, while she passes out of the room, leaving the words ringing in his ears,—"just a few minutes, old goosey, until I put baby to bed."

When she returns she has changed her attire. If she was beautiful before she is simply ravishing now. The old man is bewildered by her charms. Ere he knows it he finds himself relieved of coat and vest and his feet encased in slippers.

An hour elapses.

What is that? A violent ringing at the doorbell.

"My God! my husband!"

With disheveled hair, disarranged attire, and a face as pale as death the pretty woman drops to her feet. Her wretched companion is nearly frightened out of his wits.

"What shall I do?" he gasps.

She shoves him into a closet, and then, controlling herself with an apparent effort, hastens to let her liege lord and master in. She opens the door and the next instant is clasped into the arms of her husband. Their lips meet in a long lingering kiss.

"Oh, my darling, I am so glad that you are back!"

"And are you glad to see me, dear?"

"Oh, so much!"

He kisses her again, and says:

"What a dear, true little wife I've got."

Finally the innocent and unsuspecting husband is sent into the kitchen. As soon he disappears she darts into the room where she has left her aged mash. With a rapidity that is astonishing, she rifles his pockets. After which she lets the trembling wretch out of the closet, thrusts his clothes into his arms and literally forces him into the street, crying:

"Fly! fly for your life! my husband!"

And he flies—flies, not on the wings of love but of fear—flies until he reaches a dark and secluded corner where he commences a violent can-can struggle with his garments.

In the meantime a strange scene is transpiring in the house. Our beautiful heroine is again clasped in her loving husband's arms.

Both are laughing immoderately. She holds up a wallet before his pleased eyes.

"How much?" he asks.

"Five hundred!" she returns with a sweet little gurgle. Oh! wasn't he sucker!"

And this is the adventuress of the Ferry boat.

CHAPTER II.

A Gay But Sinful Life.

SHE was a slashing beauty with a figure that was symmetry itself. .

Her eyes were black as coals and her complexion was a beautiful pink and white.

And she could put her dainty slippered foot on a chandelier in a way that would astonish the oldest bald-headed patron of the theater.

Pretty, vivacious and attractive, is it strange that she had her admirers?

She was called Pauline, and sometimes only plain Poll.

Pauline delighted in being known as a high-flyer. She could break a bottle of wine and smoke a cigarette in the most astonishing manner. On Sunday afternoon during the warm weather, she would drive out to Grosse Pointe with one of her numerous lovers, and "blow herself" like a millionaire.

And the "boys" all said—"now there is the kind of people to travel with." And all the bloods in town fought to "travel" with her, too.

Pauline got boiling full one night and put her foot through the window of a coupe. The driver endeavored to expostulate with his intoxicated passenger, and she at once planted her jeweled fist into one of his "peepers."

A policeman, at this interesting juncture, put in appearance, and Pauline finished the night in the old Woodbridge street station.

When she faced the Police Justice the next morning, her countenance looked "beery" and her hair was disheveled, but her elegant attire to some extent balanced these defects in her appearance.

Pauline felt somewhat abashed at her surroundings but she determined to put on a bold front knowing that she had money in her possession. Leaning on the railing in an attitude decidedly picturesque, she calmly said:

"Well, what's the damage?"

The judge smiled, and turning to the policeman who made the arrest, he said in his calm, dignified manner:

"Officer, raise your right hand and be sworn."

When the latter had given his testimony, His Honor said:

"Well, Pauline, what have you to say for yourself?"

"Oh, nothing," the fair but frail prisoner returned, lifting her eyebrows with amusing indifference.

The fine was $5 with the alternative of 20 days in the House of Correction. She paid the fine.

When Pauline rejoined her female associates that day she recounted the scenes she had gone through with much amusement. She laughingly told how she struck the coupe driver, and reiterated with some exageration, her conduct while on trial. She was the heroine of the hour.

Fair Pauline! Alas! It was not long ere the beautiful roses in her cheeks began to fade, the lilies in her brow to droop and wither—the cold, cruel frost of adversity was nipping them in the bud. The drugs of the apothecary could not disguise this fact long and the features once so fair to look upon, soon lost their youthful bloom.

But her voice rang out as loud and merry as ever, and her spirits lost none of their gaity or vivaciousness.

But the brightest day must have an ending. And the sunshine of this young but sinful life soon passed into the dark clouds of misfortune.

Down! down! she went from one grade of prostitution to another. It is strange how rapidly these women fall when once their beauty begins to fade. And this case was no exception.

One day the body of a woman was fished out of the river. A crowd of men. who were lounging about the dock, gathered around the remains. When the Coroner arrived he said:

"Who is she, boys?"

No one answered. Finally a trampish looking individual with a fiery red nose and bleary eyes, stepped forward; and after carefully examining the cheap calico dress that shrouded the figure, he said:

"I knows her, boss."

"And who is she?"

"Te-he!" grinned the fellow, with a hideous expression on his countenance. "She was once my woman. I was her lover boss! I knows her by the calico dress."

"Her name?"

"Poll, boss, but wunst, when she was a high-flyer, they called her Pauline."

Alas! poor Pauline! Vain, foolish woman! With her beauty and accomplishments her life might have been a different one.

Yet probably she was not alone to blame. Her own true, loving, confiding nature might have been the cause of her ruin and distruction—but the story of the unfilled promise need not be told again.

We only know a villian lives and a woman is dead. One is known to-day by his wealth happiness and gilded surroundings, while the other—poor Pauline! how is she known? Alas! only by the rags that cover her lifeless remains!

CHAPTER III.

The Bewitching Book Agent.

Oh, the cars! the cars!
  The noisy, rattling railroad cars;
How they jumble,
    Rumble,
      Grumble,
Or unexpectedly take a tumble,
And fire a fellow unaware,
  Like a catapult through the air,
While his low and desperate swear,
  Glides serenely through the cars.

Oh, the dust! the dust!
  The dirty, awful railroad dust!
It settles sweetly,
    Neatly,
      Discreetly,
On the traveler completely,
And the temperature of the air
  Grows decidedly heated where
The martyred passengaire
  Is seated in the cars.

Oh, the grub! the grub!
  The hashy, mashy railroad grub!
It's a daisy,
    Hazy,
      Mazy,
It will make you crazy,
And if you can down it when
  The conductor, in less than minutes ten,
Shouts "all aboard," why then
  You should travel on the cars.

IF THE gentle reader will permit I will refer to the above as an attempt at rail-lery! I might use a far more appropriate word, but then the opportunity is irresistable, and besides in a person of my train-ing——enough! I will be more car-ful. I was about to remark that the above attempt at raillery was written

" Would you like a Carriage "

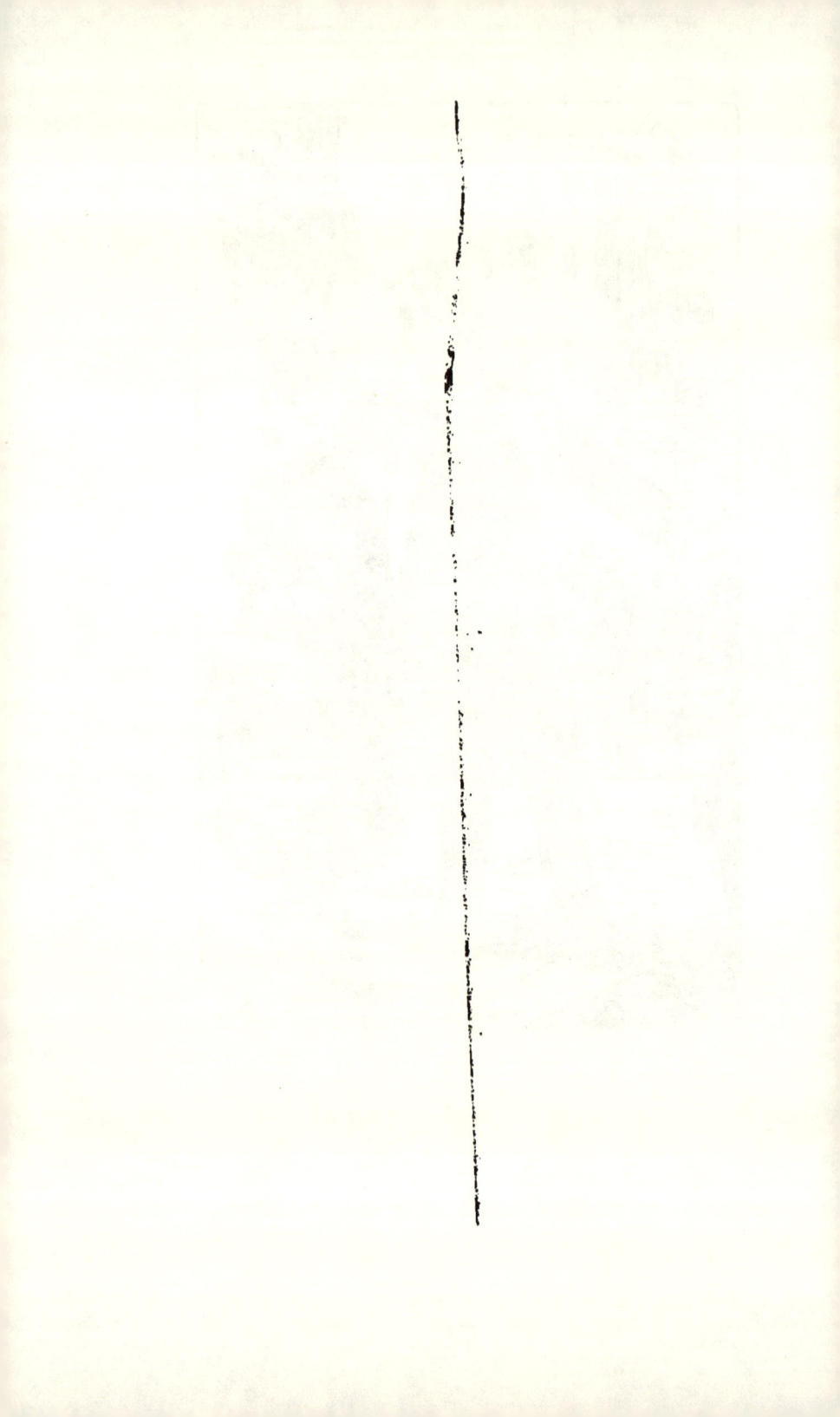

while traveling on a railroad train between Grand Rapids and Detroit last summer. I had an adventure on the same train of a rather remarkable character, which may be worth telling.

⁎

It was a warm, sultry day and the dust and dirt blew through the railroad coaches very much like the sand which you have seen portrayed in the pictures of the Sahara desert.

It was something terrible!

I was wrapped up in a long linen duster, and I undoubtedly presented a very unhappy picture with the perspiration running down in rivulets through the dust on my face. I sighed as I thought of my appearance, and I sighed because of my uncomfortable position, and I sighed for a glimpse of the depot at Detroit.

I do not know whether it was because of my sighing or not, but my attention was finally drawn by two big dark eyes looking at me in the most questioning manner from the seat in front, and the eyes belonged to one of the most beautiful girl faces I had seen in a long while. I ceased my sighing and dropped down into the depths of my duster, where I remained several minutes quietly thinking of the pretty face in front of me.

She was alone and this fact encouraged me to hope that I might possibly make her acquaintance, so I pulled myself into shape and leaned forward, patiently awaiting an opportunity.

Finally she turned. Our eyes met. She smiled. So did I. I was more successful than I had dared to wish.

"Is it not warm?" I politely remarked, half in statement and half in interrogation.

"Is it?" she replied with such cold indifference that my enthusiasm received a very abrupt and startling check.

I fell back into my seat again and as I mopped the perspiration from my face I replied with some desperation.

"Well, by sheol! I should say so!" and then I relapsed into a silence, mentally cursing my stupidity and forwardness. As I sat in my seat I found myself studying the back of her head, her shoulders and her bonnet, and she wore the dearest little bonnet I have ever seen. I never could describe it, and therefore will not try. To me it

was simply a pleasing, bewitching miscellany of colors,
ribbons and flowers.

A long, loud whistle from the engine proclaimed the
fact that we were approaching a station.   The train
slacked up, and the brakeman shouted something like this
at the door,

"Po-o-o-ack!"

The unfortunate individual was trying to say Pontiac!

When we left Pontiac the little lady was still seated in
front of me, and what pleased me more she appeared to
look somewhat kindlier in my direction.

As I said before it was unusually warm in the cars,
and the heat and the close atmosphere was making me
disagreeably sleepy.   My chin was falling on my breast
and a million bonnets were dancing a sort of can-can in
my uncertain vision, when suddenly—

"Nice, fresh, roasted peanuts!   Will you have some
sir?   Only five cents a glass."

I awoke with a start, and probably would have made
some violent answer had I not noticed that the young lady
in front was looking into the man's peanut basket with
rather wistful eyes.   I at once perceived another open-
ing to her acquaintance and I determined to try again.

I purchased some peanuts and while doing so politely
asked her if she would have some.   She laughed lightly,
and as a tiny flush stole over her cheeks, she replied:

"Just a few, please."

I was so completely paralyzed by her answer that I
might not have paid the man for his goods had he not
quietly reminded me that I had forgotten something.

But the acquaintance was begun and I was not a man
to allow it have only a beginning.   To tell the truth we
got on in the most agreeable manner and even went so far
as to squeese each other's hands.

We were a few miles from Detroit when my little companion slyly whispered.

"Tell me your name again."

I did.

She looked up roguishly at me, and said:

"I never could remember that.   Write it here, will
you please?"

She held a little paper in her hand, and in such a position I could see only a small portion of it.

I took out my pencil and said:

"Let me take the paper?"

"I cannot," she returned, looking at me with her dark eyes, "its a private letter. Wait until we become better acquainted."

She held out the paper and I complied with her request, for which she thanked me kindly.

In the depot at Detroit I held her hand and said earnestly:

"I hope we may meet again."

And in just as earnest a manner she replied:

"I hope so."

I looked at her quickly. Was there something meant in her inflected utterance.

She divined my thoughts, for she replied:

"Do you know what you signed?"

"What—when?" I gasped.

"That paper on the cars," she replied, with a malicious little chuckle.

"What?"

"A contract for a $15-book to be paid on the installment plan! I am a book agent."

Before I could reply she darted out of my sight among the throng in the depot and was gone.

CHAPTER IV.

The Heartless Procurer.

THE train over the Michigan Central had just run into the depot, the engine was puffing and gasping as if affected with asthma, a number of bells were ringing and clanging in the most discordant and deafening manner, and hundreds of people were darting to and fro. The passengers from the train were rushing one way and the railroad employes another and consequently there were many sudden and violent collisions. But all seemed to take it in good part.

The majority of the faces wear a light, happy and expectant look. They are returning home—home sweet home! and soon they will be clasped in the arms of loving and devoted relatives and true and tried friends. How fast our feet carry us on such occasions!

Here a young and affectionate wife is found kissing a husband, who has been absent from the city; here an old grey-haired mother, her pale and seared cheek bedewed with fast-falling tears, rests her weak and trembling body against her sturdy son, who has been away braving the world alone; here are greetings of brothers, sisters sweethearts and all those who are linked to humanity by the sacred bonds of love, affection or friendship.

It is here we are not ashamed of those tender or sentimental parts of our nature. Mock-modesty is thrown aside and our truer and better nature is revealed.

At the gates stand the phlegmatic and dignified police officers. The crowd hasten by them and pour into the street and then follows the clamor and cries of the hackmen.

Some take carriages, others hasten towards the street cars, while still others are satisfied to continue their journey afoot.

The very last of the passengers is a sweet, innocent-faced young girl. Her dress is neat but poor and her appearance at once proclaims that she is strange to city life.

She looks pale and frightened and does not seem to know which way to turn.

At that moment a young man steps up to her.

"Would you like a carriage?" he asks in his most persuasive manner.

"No, sir; I have only to go around the corner, thank you!"

"If you have no objections I will escort you to the corner."

"You are so kind!"

"Not at all. You will never be able to go pass all those men."

He leads the way and she follows. They engage in conversation, and the poor, innocent little child, ere she is aware of it, tells her story.

She had read in silly books how young girls come to large cities and make fortunes. No; she did not expect to make a fortune (demurely) but had simply come to find work.

Work? Why he knew just the place. A splendid situation with hardly anything to do and lots of money.

They stop in front of a large brick house. It is the very place he was speaking of. She hesitates, but it is only for a moment. She recollects his bright words and a reassuring look settles the matter.

She goes like a lamb to slaughter!

The procurer has done his work!

And the victim has been trapped!

A little drugged wine or coffee accomplishes the rest.

Many a poor young country lass has been lead into the broad and inviting pathway of sin in this manner.

CHAPTER V.

The Lady Masseuse.

JUST off from Woodward avenue, on a certain thoroughfare, there stands a pretty cottage, with a big bay window just peeping through a great mass of creeping vines. The cottage is a short distance back in the yard. Numerous dainty flower beds bedeck the grounds, and beautiful shade trees cast their cool and agreeable shadows.

An air of mystery surrounds the house and its occupants. The place is always so quiet that the observing passer-by is at once struck with the appearance of loneliness. Faces are rarely, if ever, seen at the windows. When the door is opened to admit callers, a colored man may be seen in the hallway.

And who are the callers? They generally appear to be men past the prime of life; their grey hair, sober and measured walk and broadcloth bespeak men of good position in the financial world.

A gentleman, whom for convenience I shall term Slicktalker a somewhat suggestive name by the way, took occasion to investigate the interior of this place. The door was opened as usual by the colored attendant. "My name is Mr. Slicktalker," said the visitor. "I was referred to this place by Mr. Blank," mentioning a gentleman whom he had seen visiting the house.

The colored man bowed graciously and led Mr. Slicktalker into the parlor, where he was soon met by a very beautiful woman, with lustrous eyes, and a magnificent figure, which was shown to advantage by her wearing apparel. She smiled sweetly, displaying an even row of white, pearly teeth.

"Good day, monsieur," and the visitor knew that she was French, "you wish to take a massage treatment?"

Mr. Slicktalker answered in the affirm attire.

"What is the price?" asked Mr. Slicktalker.

"Three dollars," returned the lady, in her most bewitching manner.

"I have never gone through the experience, do you know, and—"

"You will like it, monsieur. You cannot help but like it," interrupted the woman with sparkling eyes.

Mr. Slicktalker thought he would. How could he help but like it, and especially when such a charming woman had assured him that it would be pleasurable to him?

Mr. Slicktalker was relieved of his hat and cane and ushered into another apartment, the gorgeousness of which made him think he was in an eastern seraglio. It was a large room and furnished up with a seeming disregard of cost. Handsome divans and easy chairs were on every hand. The furniture was of the most costly black mahogany. Beautiful Turkish rugs were placed in front of the divans. The panes in the windows were of stained glass, and the light entered the apartment through the glass and lace curtains in a manner peculiarly pleasant to the eyes.

The light was dim and low; the atmosphere warm, yet not unpleasant, and made sensual by rich and agreeable eau de cologne.

Mr. Slicktalker, although a man of the world, was much astonished. He could say but little! But his astonishment was destined to increase.

"If monsieur will step into the adjoining apartment he can disrobe. You will find a pair of tights which you will put on."

Mr. Slicktalker immediately disappeared into the adjoining room. When he returned he was dressed in a short pair of tights. The room had been made darker, and objects were not so clear to the eyes.

"Step this way," said a sweet young voice.

Mr. Slicktalker glanced in the direction of the voice. He was looking at a beautiful young girl, who was attired like a ballet dancer.

And the massage treatment was begun.

Does the gentle reader know what the massage treatment is?

The masseuse is invariably a woman. She seizes and squeezes after a peculiar fashion each tired muscle, until all soreness or weariness of the body and mind disappears, and perfect rest and comfort follows.

Ostensiby the massage is what might be termed a medicinal luxury, but in many cases the surroundings are such as to lure both manipulator and subject beyond the boundary line of decency. Recently the Cincinnati detective department brought a series of investigations to a climax by raiding the leading massage establishment of that city. The proprietress and two female assistants were arrested and held to the charge of indecent behavior.

CHAPTER VI

The Beautiful Opium Smoker.

"OH! GOD! the misery, the sorrow and the shame that are mine!"

With a low, pitious wail the wretched creature buried her pale, wan face, in her hands, and rocked her body to and fro.

It was a strange, interesting scene—a scene which at a single glance revealed a sad but terrible story—a story of the ruined and wrecked life of a weak and unfortunate woman.

The miserable apartment was dimly lighted by a lamp, which threw out a disgusting smell of oil. A couple of cots or trunks were in the room.

But in strange contrast with the place was the woman, who uttered the exclamation that opened this chapter. Her attire proclaimed her a person of no insignificent means. She wore a magnificent sealskin sack and diamonds sparkled on her hands and ears.

Finally she looked up, and then it was seen how beautiful she was. Her face, in spite of the sad careworn look, was remarkably attractive. The eyes, large, black and lustrous, were fringed with long, dark lashes.

But the deathly whiteness of her complexion, without a particle of coloring, looked more like polished, transparent Parian marble than human flesh. The woman was beautiful, yet she possessed that style of beauty that we admire but cannot love. The face was too cold, passionless and indifferent.

The door was suddenly thrown open and a Chinaman, attired in the dress peculiar to his countrymen, entered the apartment. He carried a long pipe in his hand.

From the bowl, bluish colored smoke circled toward the ceiling, and the peculiar aroma in the room became stronger and still more sickening.

The woman's face brightened up in a remarkable manner at the entrance of the Chinaman. She reached out her hand, which trembled with eagerness, and seized the pipe.

"Smookee?" said the Chinaman, with a grin that made his ugly face, fairly hideous.

"Yes! yes!" cried the woman, with nervous impatience.

She placed the pipe between her lips while the Chinaman slunk back into the shadows of the room where his little, round eyes gleamed and danced in the darkness.

The above scene was transpiring in one of the numerous opium joints that infest this beautiful city. The woman in question was the wife of a well known and prominent traveling man, whose work compelled him to be absent from home the greater portion of the time. He little knew of the terrible vice with which his wife had become afflicted. But the awful revelation was to come to him only too soon.

One night he returned home unexpectedly, and arrived just in time to see his wife departing. A strange impulse prompted him to follow her, which he did. He was doomed to the greatest surprise in his life.

The woman proceeded on her way until she reached East Larned street in the neighborhood of Randolph. She was then in the most disreputable section of that thoroughfare. Finally she turned into a laundry. The husband came up and in a quivering voice said:

"What can she be doing in there at this time of the night?"

He waited nearly fifteen minutes, and being unable to endure the surprise longer, he rushed into the place, not stopping until he reached a rear apartment.

A terrible sight met his gaze.

It was more like an awful nightmare than anything else. He could scarcely believe his senses. He staggered back and reeled like a drunken man.

His wife, a woman whom he adored as much as his very life, was reclining in a half insensible condition on a low filthy couch, while bending over her, with his hand on her necklace, was a villianously ugly Chinaman. The woman was in such a state of stupification that she did not look up.

The celestial on the contrary, was nearly frightened out of his wits. The enraged husband could control himself no longer. With a bound like a panther he leaped on the Chinaman and felled him to the floor with a sledge-hammer-like blow. Then he lifted his wretched wife in his arms and carried out on the street. A carriage conveyed her to her home.

And what was the result?

The unfortunate and miserable woman is now an inmate of the Pontiac Insane Asylum, while her husband mysteriously disappeared from the city and has not been heard from since.

The opium mania!

No one knows the full and awful import of these words, but those people who are addicted to the terrible vice. Opium smoking and opium eating have been but recently, comparatively speaking, introduced into America, but the habit is gaining ground with terrible rapidity.

To-day all the large cities in the United States have their "opium joints." These are generally run by Chinese.

Opium eating and smoking are carried on to an alarming extent in Detroit, and the victims of this awful vice are increasing in number almost daily. The Chinese laundries hold the principal patrons of the opium habit.

And how many people are addicted to the opium habit in Detroit?

It has been variously estimated. Some people have placed the figure at 2,000!

Two thousand of people in Detroit gradually killing themselves by this most pernicious of vices. The assertion is most startling, and the need of some stringent measure to stay the advance of the awful habit is most manifest.

The opium joint proprietor carries on his nefarious business in Detroit in the most serreptitious and careful manner, and it is almost impossible to locate. him. He is very guarded, too, about his patrons, and none are tolerated in his place but those in whom he imagines he can place the most implicit confidence.

CHAPTER VII

Scenes at Arbeiter Hall.

ARBEITER HALL!
This great resort for our German population is one of the institutions of the city.

But the luster and glory of Arbeiter Hall are gradually passing away.

A few years ago this place used to be a veritable bedlum where the devotees of Gambriunus and Terpsichore turned out to "blow in" the night.

But an old-time dance is now the exception rather than the rule.

Now and then of a Saturday night, however, a dance is given at this place which is a reminder of days gone by.

Beer flows like water and everybody goes in for a great time.

The saloon is crowded with men and women, and the latter "hold up the bar" and sit on the beer tables just as "regular" as their male companions.

The dances at Arbeiter Hall are run on the free-and-easy plan. There is little ceremony there. All go in for a good time.

And they get it.

One of the features of Arbeiter Hall is the bouncer. He is necessarily a big fellow with muscles like those of John L. Sullivan. He is supposed to drink more beer and strike the hardest blow of any man in the house.

He's a dandy.

At least he thinks he is.

He stands on guard near the door and awaits developments. He has not long to wait.

I tell you the bouncer earns his money. There is no mistake about that. His position is no sinecure.

Trouble is brewing. An intoxicated man has just left the bar room and is staggering into the ball. He approaches a young woman who is hanging on the arm of a male companion.

"How to do, daisy," he cries.

The next instant he is sitting on his head and making a vain endeavor to disentangle his legs from his neck. On the refined and elegant language of the prize ring, he has been "smashed in the jaw."

"Fight! Fight!" yell the crowd.

Great consternation prevails. The women glance curiously on while the men prepare for battle.

"Rous mit em!"

"Rous mit em!"

The war cry of Arbeiter Hall has been sounded.

"Rous mit em" means blood every time.

The bouncer has leaped from his position at the door. He jumps into the middle of a crowd which had quickly gathered around the fallen man. He espies the fellow who had delivered the blow and the next instant the two have grappled together. Then friends of both men takes sides.

Biff! Bang!

"Go for him!"

"Sock it to him!"

"Plug it to him, old man!"

"Rous mit em!"

Pandemonium reigns supreme. The scene that ensues baffles description.

A crowd of men are slugging one another regardless of whom they hit. It is a melee after the most approved Irish pattern.

Everybody joins in.

Even the women take a hand in when the opportunity presents itself.

The air is burdened with beer glasses and flying hats.

The bouncer at last floors his man. He is breathing heavily and his face is covered with blood. His shirt collar hangs on the back of his neck.

But the other fellow is a sad looking wreck. He is

demoralized as well as demolished.   His face and clothes
are smeared with blood.

The bouncer grasps him by the coat-collar and drags
him towards the door. The crowd then surge in that
direction still yelling and fighting with all their might.

The door is thrown open.

The eventful moment has arrived.

"Rous mit em!"

The next instant several men are thrown bodily down
the stairway. It is a wonder they are not killed.
Another gang seize them on the floor below and they are
given a final shove into the street. After which they are
gathered in by the policeman on the outside and carted
away to the police station.

In the meantime the crowd on the inside have become
quited down again. The music starts up and couple after
couple whirl merrily away out on the smooth shining
floor. The dancers gradually increase in number until it
is impossible to cross the hall.

And the bouncer, proud, magnificent and glorious,
hangs over the lager beer bar, "downing" the beer in the
most startling fashion. Admiring friends stand around
him and loudly extol his qualities as a slugger, while he,
modest fellow that he is, softly remarks: "When they
gets the best of me they'll have to get up early in the
morning; now I am speaking, I am!"

Observe that couple at one of the tables. The man is
boiling over, and the fair young damsel, sitting on his
knee, delights in pulling his hat down over his eyes.

And she ought to hide his face.

The man is a big government official, and has a beautiful young wife and children. He moves in the highest
circles of society, and yet he is so drunk that it would be
impossible for him to walk without assistance.

His companion is a notorious woman of the town.

What would his wife, his children, or his hightoned
friends say if they could see him now?

But they wont see him. His female friend will look
out for that. She will lose nothing by it either.

The next day, when he awakes, he finds himself in
strange apartments and there is a splitting paine in his
head. After liquidating his bill he is let stealthfully out
of a side door.

He does not rest until he gets a cocktail and shampoo. Then he goes home and does the old time song and dance act to his dear little wife. And she, poor, deluded, foolish thing that she is, pats him on the cheek, and says:

"Poor fellow! you are being worked nearly to death! you need a good long rest!"

But to Arbeiter Hall again.

The music is playing louder and faster now. The dancers have lost their agility and gracefullness and collisions are of common occurrence. They are getting full! Men are calling across the hall and the loud ringing laughter of the women tell that the liquor is beginning to manifest itself.

In the bar room men and women are stretched out on chairs; others are staggering aimlessly around, while standing up to the bar is the loud mouthed, jesticulating would-be fighter, making himself as obnoxious and disgusting as he possibly can; just back of him is an individual, whose countenance is the picture of imbecility as he endeavors to trill forth some Baccanalian song. It is a scene of carousing and drunkenness that cannot be easily described.

Late Sunday morning a gang of weak-kneed loud-mouthed men and women tumble out of Arbeiter. The rising sun is already streaking the eastern skies.

"Oh, we wont go home till morning,
   We wont go home till morning,
   We wont go home till morning,
      Till daylight does appear!"

CHAPTER VIII.

Police Court Habitues.

THE Detroit Police Court!
It's a daisy!
And every Monday morning you can catch it in full bloom.

While its aroma would drive the small-pox out of a Polish settlement.

There is nothing like it in the world.

Here is where the changes are rung on humanity in the most bewildering manner.

It is a heterogeneous mass of foul-smelling, ill-shaped, distorted ragged, wretched humanity, and it is parceled out in all sizes, shapes and colors.

And the lobby.

It would make an owl laugh.

The red-nosed, beetle-browed, ragged clothed lobby— but what would the Police Court be without the lobby?

The judge might be just as well disposed of. The moment the doors are opened the shivering, filthy crew rush pell-mell into the courtroom as though their very lives depended on their gaining entrance.

Then there is the judge himself, tall, calm, dignified and handsome. When he enters the courtroom the silence is like death. Hats are suddenly jerked off and the motly crowd is the picture of humility and attention.

The court officers sit erect, those standing throw back their shoulders and a ferocious frown darkens the mammoth brow of the court crier.

It is a chilling scene and all levity is quickly coated with ice. The court crier raises the gavel and then brings it down with a terrific bang.

"Order!" he yells.

And the judge ascends the bench. After becoming seated he dampens his lips with ice water, and says:

"Call the cases."

"Abner Logan!"

A burley policeman suddenly shoves a middle-aged "coon" forward.

"Abner, are you here again?" sternly.

"Yes, sah, sullenly.

"What have you been doing now?"

"I dunno."

"You don't know."

"No, sah."

"Been fighting?"

"I dunno."

"He has Your Honor, why he nearly murdered another colored man," put in the policeman.

"Do you hear that, Abner?"

"He dun gon an' tell a lie, jedge."

"Abner, I am getting tired of sending you to the works. We will now change the sentence. You can go!"

He went.

"Delia Miner!"

A dusky damsel ambled forward and made a low courtesy to His Honor.

"Drunk again, eh?"

"Jedge—

"Five dollars or twenty days."

"But jedge—

"Here! here!" howled one of the court officers, grabbing the woman and hustling her out of the courtroom in a jiffy.

"And your name is John Brown?" said His Honor to the next prisoner.

The prisoner made a profound bow with one hand on his breast.

"You look like a chronic. Are you a chronic?"

"I am an unfortunate victim—

"Ha-Ha! I am on to you like a wolf! You are one of the spring time gentle Annie chronics, you want to go up for several months so when you get out the flowers will be blooming in the spring tra-la-la! Well I've got you down for three months. Never mind thanking me, good-bye!"

"Your Honor" said the next prisoner, making a military salute, "I must acknowledge that I am rather stuck on your conntenance."

"You make me feel silly," said the judge.

"You remind me of my old general in the war."

"Are you a weather-beaten son of Mars?"

"I am an old campaigner."

"Well, gather up your goods and chattels and double quick march.

He marched.

A woman with a woe-begone looking countenance, draped with two black eyes, made a desperate attempt to smile sweetly on His Honor when the name Annie Flynn was called.

"Annie," said the judge in a meditative manner, "you are looking unusually tough this morning.

"Yes your Highness."

"You look like a tea store chromo that had seen hard usage."

"Yes your Lordship."

"Have you been wrestling with a lamppost or the gutter, Annie?"

"I can't say, your Worship."

"Very well, you will soon join that unfortunate visitor at this court, the famous Mary Jane Comber, if you do not mend your ways. You had better wrestle with work-house hash instead of gutters and side-walks. Twenty days or five dollars."

"Bridget Rush!"

An aged woman with a red nose and green veil was waltzed forward. A sad weary expression stole over the judge's countenance.

"Bridget, will you ever stop drinking?"

"Now your Honor knows—

"Now don't work that old gag on me again. I have heard that so often I dream of it at night time. You were out visiting and you happened to drop in and see a lady, and — and — well don't, I call the turn on you?"

Bridget glanced toward the floor but said nothing.

"Bridget," said the judge, with a melancholy air, "I have come to look on you as my mascot. If you happened to drop out— go to that bourne where the wicked cease from troubling and the weary are at rest; in fact join the great majority, a huge, black cloud would dim my judicial career forever more and I believe I would throw up the sponge in this struggle for earthly existance."

Bridget sobbed audibly and the old, faded, red shawl, which had done so much service in the past, brushed away the tears that welled in her eyes.

"Bridget, can your mind revert to the long ago — to childhood's happy days? Do you see again the old home, the rippling stream and the green meadow? Do you remember when your complexion was like the lilies and the blue of heaven shone in your eyes?"

Bridget sobbed louder and buried her tear-stained face in the shawl.

"Alas! Bridget, time has not dealt kindly with you, or you have not dealt kindly with yourself. Your hair is growing gray, your face is blotched and red and there is a bad hacking cold on your chest. Hesitate, Bridget, ere you tumble into the bottomless and awful depths of eternity."

His Honor wrote a few lines on the court docket.

"You cannot care for yourself, Bridget, and I shall be compelled to put you into the hands of others who will care for you."

Bridget raised her red and swollen eyes while the judge said:

"Five dollars or thirty days!"

CHAPTER IX.

Gambling.

OW does he stand now, pard?"

"Nearly three thousand ahead of the bank."

"He is cool."

"Yes, but Howard looks pale."

"Well, he ought to. What's big winning, that is, and more than has been taken from one house in a long while."

"He is in big luck.

"Never saw such luck."

The words were uttered in Billy Howard's elegant and quiet gaming rooms known as "The Owl." They were the whispered remarks of two men standing close together. They were a few feet away from a table where a man was playing faro.

This man was large and well built with a heavy blonde mustache. There was nothing particularly flashy about his appearance. His manner was unusually calm and collected. His movements slow, almost sluggish. His appearance was not that of the book gambler; it was that of the gambler seen in real life.

Again he played. Again he won. Would fortune never desert him? It seemed not.

The dealer bit his lips. The blood shot from his face. He was growing rattled by the remarkable run of luck of the player.

Such luck had rarely, if ever, been witnessed before in a Detroit gambling house. The man had been playing a day and a half.

In this time he had won nearly $3,000.

Howard finally left the place evidently thinking that his presence was his own Jonah. Sporting men are superstitious. Once on the street he hastily sought something to drink. The cold fresh air braced him up and the liquor steadied his nerves.

The dapper little fellow laughed at his own ill-luck and his handsome face became wreathed in smiles.

Turning to a gentleman he said:

"I have left a man up at my place playing faro. When I return he will probably own the house.

He had scarcely set his glass on the counter when a blonde man entered the saloon. It was the lucky gambler.

The two shook hands and drank together.

"Billy" said the blonde man, "I think of going up north to go into business."

"You had better stick to bank," said Howard with a cough.

"I hope you don't feel discouraged?"

"Not at all. All that I want is your game. I will get even in the long run.

"You can have my game old man. I will play in your place every time I come to town. I had no luck in Weithoff's. I have lost $10,000 in that place. You are in tough luck, but it can't always last. You will make it out of me the next time."

"All that I want is your game."

"And you can have it."

Howard's loss quickly spread among sporting men. It was rumored that he had been broken up, and that a "chump" gambler had "turned the box" and "busted" the "bank."

But the reports were far from correct. It will take a much greater loss than $3,000 to break up Bill Howard's bank.

And who was this lucky individual? He is well known in the local gambling houses. He has lost and won considerable money in Weithoff's. A while ago he did the baby act and sued Weithoff for some money which he claimed to have lost gambling. That is why they call him a "chump" gambler.

A sport always sizes up such men with disdain. Their idea is that a man who kicks when he is done up in a gambling house is no good. His intention is to do up the house, and when he gets the worst of it he has no person to blame but himself.

But the man's luck was really something remarkable. He struck Detroit strapped. He had not a cent in his pocket. He went to a well-known sporting man and asked for the loan of $10.

"I don't know," said the sporting man, "why don't you borrow money from the men where you play your game?"

"I would rather borrow the money from you, and I promise you that I will play my game with you in the future."

"Well, all right, old man," and the ten dollars were passed over.

He returned the money, but on the trifling sum he had won nearly $3,000. He was truly in luck.

One night I walked into a gambling house. There was the usual scene: players pale, nervous and excited, dealers calm, smiling and confident and colored waiters moving noislessly about.

"Pardner, that is the last ten cents I have to my name."

The words were addressed to me. The speaker looked discouraged and disheartened. Despair was written on every lineament of his countenance.

"Play the three aces," I said.

He did so, complying mechanically.

The dice reached the table. The box was turned.

A low gasp escaped from the player's lips. The dealer uttered an exclamation of astonishment.

The three aces turned up.

He had won.

Three aces paid 180 to 1.

He had won $18 on ten cents.

A trembling hand was extended, which I grasped, and a quivering voice said:

"Stranger, may God bless you! you have saved my life!"

He said no more but took the money he had so suddenly won and made for the street.

Detroit may not be Baden Baden or Monaco but just the same a great deal of money changes hands here in gambling. At the present writing I am confident that this city does more gambling than any other place in America any where near its size. New sporting houses are being opened almost weekly, and gamblers and sporting men are flocking here from Chicago, Cincinnati, Louisville and from many of the eastern cities.

There are some really fine gambling houses here— houses with gilt-edged trappings, colored servants, perfumed air, glittering chandeliers, fizzing champagne, and— that which tells the story more than anything else—where big money is won and lost.

9

CHAPTER X.

"*Potomac*" Horrors.

HE POTOMAC!
Once upon a time, and not so long ago either, the Potomac was the most notorious place in the city. But time is making great changes in this locality, and many of the residents, who were responsible for its unsavory reputation, are seeking quarters elsewhere, advancing as it were with the business interests of the city, to a more central location, and to a place where the gullible pilgrim can be worked to better advantage.

But the evil is not entirely eradicated as yet. No; and it will not be for some time to come. Many of the most notorious dives still remain—remain like the fulsome sores of a departing disease. And this, too, in spite of the desperate attempts of the police to rout them out.

In these vile dens the most degraded of Detroits population are huddled together like sardines in the box; living—God alone knows how! but living never-the-less—living cancer-like fashion on that which is pure and undefiled—living on the despoliation of virtue, innocence—and even human life itself!

It is the cradle of crime and lust—the home of the thief, the assassin and the procuress—where a strange footstep suggests violence and the clink of money, the greatest of all crimes against God and man—murder!

Come with me, curious reader to the scene whereof I speak. Nay, do not hesitate—I mean in imagination not reality. The Potomac takes in that section of the city in the vicinity of the Brush Street Depot, running back a

couple of blocks and stretching some distance along the
river; Atwater and Franklin streets being the most notorious thoroughfares.

-Observe that small, rickety looking shanty. Never
mind its exact location. The out lines of the place are not
very clear or distinct in the intense darkness of the cold,
stormy wintry night, but they tell you that it is a miserable hovel never-the-less. And as far as your limited
vision goes you will see that the neighboring houses are
very similar in appearance to the place that I have drawn
your attention particularly to.

Through the tattered curtains on the windows a light
is seen, showing that some one lives within—that it is the
abode of human beings. Do not hold back. Draw up
your muffler well about your face. It will serve as a
disguise.

Tap—tap—tap!

"Come in!"

It is a woman's voice, but coarse, brusque and anything
but inviting.

Tap—tap!

"Come in I say! Can't yo' hear my invite? Wat's
ther mather with yo' ennyway? Want's ceremony does
yer?"

We open the door and enter a room, the first glimpse
of which cannot help but create a feeling of disgust and
repugnance. How cold and unhomelike it looks, a couple
of plain, wooden chairs, much worn by time and usage,
a yellow greasy table, and a stove, unpolished and resting
on bricks for legs, are the principal articles of furniture in
the room. A little lamp, with the chimney black with
smoke, is sputtering and flickering in the most dismal
manner; while the few sickly rays it casts are quickly
swallowed up by the gloom and darkness of the apartment.

The woman is alone. She sits close to the stove rocking her body and rubbing her hands in a futile attempt
to keep warm. What a wretched looking hag she is, and
the ragged shawl and the dirty, faded calico dress do not
lend additional charm to her appearance.

The face which turns up to greet us is a hard one. The
lineaments of that liquor bloated, pock-marked countenance
the blood-shot and cunning, leering eyes bespeak no
womanly feeling of love or kindness. It is a face, the

index of a heart, a cold, cruel—a heart black with evil-doing.

"Well, what do you want?"

The words are uttered with fierce emphasis and the woman's brows darken with passion.

"I knows w'at. yo' want? Oh! yo' collars are slick chaps yo are! Yo're after Bill are yo? W'ats he been doin' now? Guess he's as honest as yo' fellows any day.

"O-o-h! yo' aint collars, eh? lemme see!"

She starts to her feet and takes a penetrating glance at her visitors. Her countenance changes expression at once. She is evidently satisfied. In a curious manner she continues:

"W'ats the lay, gentlemen? Is it a crib yo' want's cracked? He-he! An' it's Bill yo're after to help eh? oh! I'm on to yo'! he-he!

"W-a-at! murder! Yo' make my blood run cold! He-he! Aint that w'ats they say in the books?

"An' so yo' want Bill. Yo'rn in a hurry an' can't wait. I'll tell yo' jest where yo'can find 'im."

She opens the door and explains where Bill can be found.

The scene shifts. A saloon on the Potomac. The hour is so late, however, the place is almost deserted. It is small and dingy. The floor is black with cigar stumps, tobacco juice and general refuse matter. The bar, which is sadly in need of paint and water, is on the verge of tottering over. The mirror is cracked and fly-specked, and across it, in big, ungainly letters, is inscribed the legion in soap "no trust." A couple of black bottles and a decayed lemon ornament the shelf.

These Potomac saloons are not very gorgeous affairs, I can assure you.

The bartender, a blear-eyed man with a red mustache, sits at a table playing cards with an individual who has the appearance of being a retired gentleman. His whole make-up has a decidedly retired or tired look. But this retired gentleman, with his damaged silk tile and seedy shining Prince Albert, we have seen too often to attract our further attention.

But here is our hero!

Look at him as he leans on his hands near the stove. He has a massive frame. The huge bull-neck is encircled

with the collar of a blue flannel shirt. The big, bony
hands, covered with red, coarse hair, is still further evidence of the man's enormous strength.

While thus absorbed in thought our hero is suddenly
disturbed by the bartender touching him on the shoulder.

"Two gent's to see you, Bill?"

He awakes with a start, and the face, which looks up,
has a half frightened, half defiant look. Our hero has not
the most prepossessing face in the world I must concede.
The short, red, shaggy beard, the small, black eyes and
low, beetling forehead do not constitute a countenance that
a young maid would coyly fondle after the manner of
"Ninon" in the opera "Nanon," when she cries with such
demure witchery:

"Oh, aint he sweet?"

No; there is nothing particularly sweet about Bill.
Not even his temper.

"What do you want?" he growls. "Got a job for me?
You have, eh! What is it? Is there big stakes in it?
There is, eh? Tell me yer figger an' if they catch me you
can put me down for the right kind of mug."

Further conversation follows, some vile liquor is in-
bibed and a meeting is arranged for the following night.
As we pass out of the door, Bill whispers to the bartender
with one finger on the side of his nose, — —

"I've got a job."

"Is it a good one?"

"We-ll!" says Bill, drawing the word out with peculiar significance. "Give me some old black stuff to-night;
I feel as if I could afford it."

And so we leave the man—or rather the monster, with
whom the commission of crime is only a question of money,
and look elsewhere. In this neighborhood can also be
found the Fagin, with his gang of juvenile thieves, the procuress, with her little girl victims, and the low, disreputable houses of prostitution with their miserable inmates;
here is gathered the very dregs of Detroit's humanity
festering as it were in a cesspool of vice, sin and crime.

CHAPTER XI.

The Market Saturday Night.

SATURDAY night at the Central Market.

It is one of the most striking and interesting scenes to be witnessed in Detroit.

The market is crowded, literally jammed, elbow room is at a premium. Men, women and children are huddled together like so many sheep in a freight car.

And the light given out from the miserable torches and lamps in the stalls, is dim indeed.

But what they lack in brilliancy they make up in smell.

And this combined with the odor from decaying fruit should make a nose, afflicted even with the worst kind of catarrh, turn up with intense disgust.

But that people continue to crowd into the market from one week's end to another, and that when they once get there, their noses retain their normal shape and position, and are not "tip-tilted like the petal of a flower," unless so constructed by nature, go to show that there must be some ulterior attraction, not manifest on first thought or observation, which draws them there.

And what can it be?

Can it be for the pennies that are likely to be saved by buying goods in so large and exclusive an emporium?

Do men and women journey all the way from their homes only to be pushed here and shoved there for the matter of a cent or two?

I hope they are not so mercenary.

And yet I very much doubt their economical thrift.

No; that is not the solution.

Here may be an exception, however.

A single exception!

I refer to that strong robust woman, so poorly clad, with the shawl drawn over her head, the features of her face so hard and severe, and carrying the large basket in her hand.

She has come to save the penny.

See how she hesitates and fingers each article before she buys, and with what reluctance she passes over the money in exchange. She cares not for the snaps and snarl, of the vender, or the impatience and insinuations of the elegantly attired lady beside her.

She is too much of a woman for that.

She is trying to stretch the hard-earned but honest pennies of her husband into dollars to satisfy the many hungry mouths and gladden the young and expectant eyes at home.

Brave, true woman!

Should we condemn her for that?

This is the single exception.

And what then is the solution?

It is hard to tell, one person goes for one reason and another for something else, and all are probably more or less drawn there to witness scenes of excitement—excitement—the gravitation center of American life.

Here is a slick young chap with natty clothes and chipper manner.

His eyes are shrewd, quick and restless.

The mustache on his upper lip is just sprouting, and the huge and startling "shiner" on his gay-colored scarf is glass.

He's a dandy.

And no one knows it any better than himself.

He pushes up against an old lady with glasses and bonnet. His hand slips into her dress pocket.

And out comes her pocketbook!

He starts to escape. But too late. The eagle eye of a police officer in citizens clothes is just behind him.

He had played his game once too often!

A loud cry of "thief" startles the crowd, and then the officer drags the writhing and wiggling youngster to the Police Station.

The commotion created in the throng subsides. Again the human current moves on, up one channel and down another, presenting as many varied and interesting views as may be seen in a kaleidoscope.

"Will you buy my flowers, sir?"

Poor child! Is she not beautiful? The blue eyes and golden hair do not belong in such humble quarters.

Sh! I will tell you a story. Let it be soft and low.

She had a sister, and just as beautiful as herself. A little older perhaps but as divine a picture as ever engraved by the Master hand.

A stranger came, he was handsome and smiling, and he bought from the pretty flower girl her boquets and nosegays.

He laughed and talked and she listened to all he said. Foolish girl!

They met clandestinely of course, and it was not long before the pretty flower girl forgot the humble stand in the market.

She went away.

And a widowed mother and a little girl at home cried and prayed for a daughter and sister who never returned.

And where was she?

In a gilded palace of sin and lust. Deserted and ruined she had no where else to go. Contrast the bold, brazen mannered creature, with the blotched and powdered face of to-day, with the shy, lily white complexioned girl of a year ago.

You would scarcely believe that they were one and the same person.

But such unhappily is the case.

"Will you buy my flowers, sir?"

The same pleading tender voice.

God bless you! of course we will!

The hours fly away.

Twelve o'clock.

The market is deserted. The lights are gone and darkness and quietness reign supreme.

A few minutes later a patrolman puts in appearance, and with slow and measured tread, he keeps a close watch for thieves and tramps.

When he turns a corner a shabby individual steals along in the darkness. He is a tramp. He is looking for shelter.

And in one of the many boxes or booths he generally finds it.

And so the night passes away, and with it its train of interesting scenes and incidents at the market.

CHAPTER XII.

A Villain in Real Life.

ES; probably I am a scoundrel!"

The speaker laughed low and sneeringly, exposing an even row of pearly white teeth behind a mustache, black as jet and neatly parted.

He was handsomely dressed and his fine, manly figure presented its best appearance.

He wore a silk hat and this with his white tie, standing collar and dark Prince Albert suit gave him a professional appearance.

The diamond on his finger sparkled gaily in the brilliant light of the apartment.

This man was to all appearances of the Caucasian race but beneath the refined and polished exterior flowed African blood.

His mother was white and his father was a mulatto.

And in consequence he might be easily mistaken for a person of French or Indian extraction.

And while he puffed away on a fragrant Havana, sipping at intervals from a mint julep, he discussed with amusing indifference and sang froid his numerous amours with white women.

White women?

Yes; white women. This man did not confine his love affairs to one color, but branched out as it were, playing for all within his reach.

And he took delight in it.

Huge delight—a delight that was simply fiendish.

"But does not your color hinder you in entrapping white women?"

"Pshaw, no! It is of advantage to me."

"How is that?"

"In several ways."

"What are they?"

"I can pass off as a foreigner. American girls just dote at foreigners. I never saw anything like it.

"And what nationality do you represent?"

"Spanish, French, and, ha-ha! I have even called myself a Prince of the Indies!"

"And these women never doubt you?"

"Never!"

"But your dress. I do not understand how you can tog out so well."

"Oh, but that is easily done."

"Yes; with money."

"Money is a mere bagatelle. Brains is all that is required. Now what would you suppose the suit of clothes that I have on now cost me?"

"Seventy-five dollars!"

"You're way off! Come again."

"Give it up."

"Well, nothing!"

"How was that?"

"I put $6 in the bank and then went to a tailor and ordered a pair of pantaloons to cost $6. When the pantaloons were done I gave him a check on the bank."

"Yes."

"He thought I had money in the bank, I went around again and ordered this suit. When it was done I gave him a check for $70 on the same bank."

"But —"

"Yes; that's what the tailor is doing, butting—butting his head against a stone wall. I have got the clothes and he has got a worthless check."

"But you're liable to be arrested."

"I will look out for that!"

He looked toward the ceiling and whistled gaily. He was in thought. Finally he said:

"I had a rare adventure the other day. I fell in with a pretty girl. After two days acquaintance, I determined to come to an understanding with her."

"Did you succeed?"

"Listen. She was a young girl and fond of dress as all women are." I said to her:

"'Come to my office at 12 o'clock to-night and I will buy you a real sealskin sacque.'

"I looked her square in the face. She returned the

"What a Beautiful Woman"

look. We understood one another. She hesitated a while and at length said: "I will come!"

"I took her to a fur store and told her to select the best sacque in the house. She decided upon one. The proprietor of the store took her address and I said:

"'Can you send this up to-morrow morning?'

"He said 'yes.' I took him aside and told him that I was on my way to the bank and on my return in twenty minutes I would hand him the money for the sacque. He was pleased as any merchant would be who had just disposed of a $150 article. He rubbed his hands and smilingly said: "'All right, sir, all right!'

"Well, you never saw a woman so pleased before in all your life!"

"Did she meet you at 12 o'clock."

"She did!"

"And you bought the sacque?"

"Pshaw! do you think I am a fool!"

He put his hand in his pocket and drew out the photograph of a young woman. It was a beautiful face and as sweet and pure looking as that of a child.

"My next victim!"

"He chuckled immoderately, stroking his mustache with one hand and holding the picture in the other.

"What do you think of her?" he asked.

"Beautiful!" I returned.

"I see we have a mutual appreciation of feminine loveliness. You admire my taste. But you should see her in life! She would send you mad! She has a figure that is divine!"

"And are you working her?"

"Yes; bumping her head."

"Bumping her head?"

"Yes; filling her pretty head with gay and gilded lies. She thinks that I am a Frenchman of means and influence."

I met her on the street. It was a handkerchief flirtation. Her parents are not rich but they are well to do. She is an ambitious little woman and I am working her accordingly. Here is a letter. You will observe that it bears the Lansing postoffice stamp."

"Yes."

He opened the letter and read it. The signature bore

the name of a state senator. The writer spoke of a young woman who had been referred to him by the colored man. He said she could be given a position and the salary would be $20 a week.

"And who is the woman?"

"The original of the photograph."

"Is it a bona-fide letter?"

"The envelope is. The letter is not."

"But the name?"

"Is forged!"

"You take desperate chances."

"I do. I was made to ruin women! I wrote to the senator for one of his bills recently introduced into the senate. By return mail I got the bill. That is how I came in possession of the envelope. I wrote the letter myself."

"And forged the name?"

"Yes!"

"You will land yourself in prison."

"Nothing venture nothing have! I will show the letter to my sweet young miss and then I will compell her to accede to my demands."

"Suppose she refuses."

"I will work the marriage racket. Here's something that will catch her."

He drew a legal document from his pocket. It bore a red seal.

"What is that?"

"It is a certificate to prove my identity."

"Your identity?"

"Yes; my uncle has just died in Cincinnati and I fall heir to $44,000."

"Lucky boy?"

"But that is only in my mind you see! I will show her the letter. It speaks of my relatives. You can rest assured that I have given them all titles. It will dazzle her eyes and then she will become easy prey!"

"And if she still resists you?"

"She will not."

"But still she may."

"I have another expedient."

"And what is that?"

"Drugged wine?"

CHAPTER XIII.

A Fair, Frail and Fickle Rose.

EAUTIFUL ROSE!
Her eyes are large and blue, her hair wavy and golden and her figure a poem of symmetry.
Sprightly, sparkling and dashing, she is the cynosure of all eyes when on the street, or at a ball or opera.

Fair and beautiful Rose.

But although fair she is frail—as frail as the delicate flower from which she derives her name.

Her admirers are countless, and she, with artless coquetry, acknowledges that it is hard for her to tell who she loves the best.

A fair, frail and fickle rose.

The young woman, although she toils not, neither does she spin, lives in an elegant suite of rooms on Miami avenue.

Her wardrobe is extensive and her dainty fingers and lily white throat sparkle with diamonds.

Her anticedents are obscure and doubtful and her own pretty lips refuse to speak of her past life.

Lately this fair woman has been pulling her matrimonial strings for all they have been worth, and the other night came a climax which is destined to rather upset her pet calculations.

The dramatis personæ in this comedy-drama are: The heroine, Miss Rose; a love-smitten youth, the son of rich parents; an enamored Bay City railroader, who is unhappily linked with another woman; and last and pro-

bably least a New York merchant, whose head is also
turned by the charms and attractions of Rose.

The young man is confident that Rose will be his
wife, the railroader has commenced proceedings for a
divorce to marry Rose, and the New York merchant's
bald cranium glistens with unusual brilliancy when he
reads the letters that tell him "yes" to his fondest hopes.
Poor deluded wretch!

The other night the railroader met Rose per agreement
in a private wine room. A bottle of champagne was
opened and the liquor had the effect of warming up their
affections to a fever heat. The impassioned Bay City man,
on the eve of their departure, could not resist the opportunity to imprint a lingering kiss on the ruby lips of his
companion. He was rudly disturbed in his momentary
experience in elysium by the waiter. The latter gentleman coughed but what good was that after he had witnessed all. These confounded fellows always come when they
are not wanted! The railroader blushed and looekd dag-
gers while the modest and embarrassed Rose could only
murmur:

"I think it is a shame that there is not more system in
this place, don't you?"

Of course he did, but he only said:

"Well. never mind. Will you go there now?"

She looked shyly towards the floor.

"Answer me; please do."

The beautiful face became suffused with crimson and
the long dark lashes touched her burning cheeks.

"I-I guess not."

"My God! do! you will drive me mad! Tell me yes.
Is it money?"

"Sir," indignantly.

"Forgive me. How can I prevail upon you to go?"

She did not answer. He drew her towards him. The
beautiful willowy form made no resistance, and he crushed
her lips beneath his own. At length she quietly but firm-
ly withdrew from his embrace. He turned around and
touched the electric button. When the waiter arrived he
ordered another bottle of champagne. When this was
drunk fair Rose was in no condition to resist his importu-
nities.

On their emerging from the restaurant a young man

might have been seen to suddenly dart back into the shadows.   His eyes glittered and his face grew as pale as death.

"It is Rose!" he cried, between his teeth.   "And my God! she is drunk!   It cannot be! no, no, it cannot be!"

A coupe was in waiting, and before the young man could catch a second glimpse of the woman's face she had disappeared into the vehicle with her companion.   And then the driver after receiving instructions from his male passenger, whipped up his horses, and the coupe went rattling away over the stone pavement.

"I will learn her character to-night!" cried the young man starting after the coupe in hot pursuit.   He proved to be a good runner and easily kept the carriage in sight. It drove up Catherine street and stopped in front of a well known assignation house.   The two passengers alighted. The driver was paid and then the man and woman hastened up the front steps.   The door was soon opened in answer to their summons, and they passed into the hallway, the door closing again behind them.

In the meantime the young man had halted on the opposite side of the street.

"Curse that woman!" he hissed.   "Who would believe this of her?   She has been acting her part well, while I have been played for all I am worth.   Who can tell what the morrow will bring forth?   Probably my father will discover all and then Canada will be the only safe place for me.   Embezzlement and forgery!   Curse her!   I would like to have my fingers around her white throat!   Curse her!"

He drew a revolver from his pocket and glanced at it in a thoughtful manner.

"I will see this thing through to-night," he finally said, with a dogged determination.

He proceeded to a corner saloon, wrote a note and had it sent to the house by a young boy.   In a few minutes the messenger returned.

"Well, what did she say?" said the young man eagerly.

"She said that you must have made a mistake; that there was no such woman in the house."

The young man contracted his brows and bit his lips. He could hardly control himself.   He handed the boy a

quarter, hastily swallowed a glass of whiskey and then
strolled angerly out of the saloon.

He made his way to the house himself, knocked at the
door and awaited an answer.   An elderly woman put in
appearance.

"Well, what do you want?" she asked.

"I want to see that young woman who entered here a
few moments ago."

"You cannot!"

"I shall!"

The two glared at one another an instant and the
woman tried to close the door.   But she was not to evade
the young man so easily.   He leaped into the hallway and
said:

"Show me that young woman or there will be hell to
pay in this shebang to-night!"

The woman was frightened at his fierce demeanor.   His
loud voice and violent manner showed that he was terribly
in earnest.

"Well, be still," she said finally.   "And I will see the
lady."

"Now you are getting sensible."

The woman, who was evidently the landlady, made no
further remark and the two proceeded upstairs.   She
knocked at one of the doors and a feminine voice responded:

"Who is there?"

"The man who sent that note."

"I wont see him."

At the sound of the woman's voice the young man
found that he had made no mistake.

"Rose, I want to see you," he said sternly.

"Yes, open the door," said her male companion savage-
ly, "I'll knock his head off!"

The door was opened.   A startling scene was the
result.

Rose, beautiful, pale and trembling, attired in nought
but her chemise, crouched near the railroader, who stood
with clinched fists and swelling breast before the enraged
young man whose revolver was leveled at the guilty pair.

"I am satisfied!" he cried, and then backed out into the
hall, while the wretched Rose swooned away on the floor.

The young man left the house and the next day a little

search and inquiry resulted in his finding out about the rich merchant at New York. He lost no time in penning a few warning words to that innocent and confiding old gentleman.

And now poor Rose is pinning for the loss of two lovers, but the bold railroader is doing his utmost to fill the void in her aching heart.

And, he aint like a man who cant do it.

CHAPTER XIV.

The Ward Politician.

THROUGH a small and dirty pane of glass a ray of sunlight slowly and stealthfully penetrated. It rested timidly on the windowsill for a moment as if fearful to go further. Finally, however, it darted toward the floor and hastily stole along until an overturned tin pail stopped its progress. Near the pail were little pools of beer which had attracted the attention of innumerable buzzing flies. The sunlight travelled over the pail and continued its journey until it reached the faded calico covering of a bed. One side of the coverlet was resting carelessly on the floor. The sunlight slowly ascended the coverlet until it brought up with an uncovered hand, dangling downwards. The hand was coarse and dirty. The sunlight crept upwards until another object impeded its progress.

It was a human head.

But the face with the low forehead, the thick, red nose, the week's growth of beard and the swollen, blotchy skin suggested the most brutal instincts. The man was asleep and breathing heavily as if under the influence of liquor.

The sunlight settled down on the ill-formed visage and warmed the inflamed and sunken eyes. The sleeper grew restless. He moved uneasily. Finally he raised one hand. A low moan escaped his lips.

"Keep still, Patrick, your father is waking up."

A little woman, pale and thin, stopped rocking in her chair, dropped her sewing in her lap, and turned her attention to a ragged little urchin playing on the floor.

"I ain't sayin' a word, ma."

"Shut up, you brat! you don't want to disturb the old man now or he will be after killin' ye !" the woman hissed.

"But the "old man" was disturbed nevertheless, and the conversation of the two only served to awaken him. He yawned once or twice and then opened his bloodshot eyes. He glanced around inquiringly until his glance rested on the boy. A scowl darkened his brow and an oath escaped his lips.

"Damn that boy?" he yelled, leaping from the bed, "must he always keep me awake !"

He seized the tin pail and hurled it with all his might at his undutiful offspring. With a cry of affright the woman jumped in front of the child. The pail struck her on the temple, stretching her helpless and bleeding on the floor. The enraged man stood over the prostrate figure with a cruel, unfeeling sneer on his lips, while the boy began screaming at the top of his voice.

"Curse yo'! yo'll always interfere will yo' !" growled the man, scowling at the insensible body before him. "And yo' little imp yo', yo're the curse of it all. I'm good 'nuff to wale yo' alive !"

The boy crouched on the floor and stifled his cries with an effort.

"None 'yer whimperin' !" snarled the man. "I've heard 'nuff. D'yo! hear ?"

He filled a dipper of water and emptied it on his wife's head. Experience had probably taught him what to do under such circumstances. The remedy, though rude and applied with an unfeeling hand, had the desired effect. She opened her eyes and her loving liege, lord and master snapped :

"What's the matter with yo' ? W'at yo're layin' there for ?"

And just as if he did not know the reason why. The wretched creature made no reply. She staggered to her feet dazed and confused and mechanically brushed down her ragged and dirty calico dress. She crossed the room and sank in a chair with the blood still dripping from the wound in her head. The boy handed his mother a towel which she took and tried to dry her face. The man stood looking moodily on.

"Say, where is my breakfast ?" he finally snapped.

"Bill, there is nothing in the house to eat," returned the woman.

"Nothing to eat? Why don't yo' buy something?"

"I have no money."

"No money? The same old story! What do yo' do with all the money I give yo'?"

"Yo' gave me a dollar last week, Bill, an' that's bin eaten up."

"A millionaire wouldn't run this shanty. I suppose I'll have to buy my breakfast."

He crushed his hat down on his head and strode towards the door. The woman glanced in a pitiful manner after him.

"Bill."

"What?"

"Aint yo' goin' to git us something to eat?"

"I dunno! I'll see!" and with this unfeeling reply on his lips he slammed the door behind him.

Bill Mulligan was a politician and a famous one—in his own estimation—and he could run a caucus as well as any man in town. Bill was a caucus or ward politician and he had considerable following among a certain class of men. Bill kept a saloon once but his inattention to business, his fondness for liquor and the high license finally brought his career as a liquor merchant to a close. Since then he has been going down lower and lower until it seemed as if his wretched life must needs soon end.

When Bill left his wife and child he was in no pleasant state of mind. His nerves were unstrung and his throat was parched and dry. Never in his life did he feel the need of whisky more than then. He shoved his hands in his pockets in vain for money. He even searched in the linings of his clothing, but with the same lack of success. He plodded on heedless as to his destination.

"Hello, Bill!"

He looked up. He recognized a familiar countenance. It was an office-seeker, and the ward politican become illumined with smiles. He extended a dirty but cordial hand, which the other grasped. They looked into one another's face. There was a mutual feeling between them.

"Bill," said the office seeker, "can I depend on you on election?"

"Can yo'? Well, now yo're humpin' yo'rself!"

Unconsciously the two walked into a neighboring saloon. They became seated, ordered drinks, and while refreshing the inner man, discussed those ponderous schemes peculiar to politicians.

Suddenly Bill Mulligan's face turned pale. The whisky glass fell to the floor and smashed into a hundred pieces. His eyes stared and his jaws dropped.

"Look! Look there! See that snake crawling beneath the bar!"

He trembled violently. There were three or four men in the barroom and they looked in the direction indicated by Mulligan's eyes.

"My God! there is another!" yelled the man, thoroughly frightened. "And another! another! They are coming in this direction!"

It was a clear case of "snakes." King Alcohol had finally mastered his victim. Mulligan would have fled from the saloon had he not been prevented. A policeman was summoned and the human wreck was taken away to the Police Station in a patrol wagon.

* * *

"He is dead!"

The white moonlight flooded a prison cell through a narrow iron-barred window. The figure of a man lay on the floor with his countenance fixed in the awful expression of death.

He was dead.

It needed not the words of the officer on duty to tell this. The fact was terribly manifest, and the trembling woman with her sobbing child, looked with streaming eyes on the wretched remains of a husband and father, and knew that he had gone to meet his Maker.

Bill Mulligan's days on earth had ended.

CHAPTER XV.

Madame Faubourg, of Petoskey.

IN the vicinity of Petoskey stands a large frame dwelling house almost hid from sight amidst the foliage of trees. The house is built after the ancient style of architecture and its many gables and latticed verandas are in keeping with the wild and rather romantic surroundings. I am going to tell you a delightful little story about this house, and for reasons which will become manifest as I proceed. I shall be compelled to use a number of fictitious instead of real names.

The first name that I shall write is Madame Faubourg. The madame is French, pretty, bewitching and at that age when ladies cease to know their years. Madame Faubourg owns the house of which I have spoken. She calls it her summer villa, and when the warm season comes on she flees from her home in Detroit and takes up her residence in this cool and invigorating climate. Then the lady orders her big, fat, liveried colored servant to open the doors, and preparations are made to receive a few boarders.

I will tell you how I became acquainted with Madame Faubourg. A short time ago I was in Traverse City, when I suddenly decided to go to Petoskey, and took the first boat to that place. A long pier runs out from the land where the boat stops. I had no sooner placed my foot on the pier when my hand was suddenly seized, and a voice exclaimed:

"My dear fellow! What brings you here? I am so glad to see you!"

I was looking into the eyes of an old schoolmate of

mine. I returned the warm pressure of hands and assured
him that our meeting could be no pleasanter to him than
to me.

"But where shall I stop?" I cried.

"I have heard both the Arlington and the Cushman
spoken of quite favorably."

"Neither," said my friend. "Now, here is a carriage,
and trust in being brought to a place where you will be
well received."

"He fairly thrust me into a conveyance standing near
and cried to the driver:

"Drive to Madame Faubourg's."   Then to me: "We
call it the Villa de Faubourg."

When we drove up to the steps of the Villa de Faubourg the door was opened by a big, fat colored servant in
livery. He took my baggage and lead the way into the
house.

A lady stood in the hallway.

"Monsieur, allow me to introduce you to Madame Faubourg," said my friend, who was at my side.

"I am pleased to meet you, Monsieur," said the lady.
"Have you come to join us in our miserable retreat?"

I took the outstretched hand, which I noticed to be unusually small and white, and remarked:

"Madame, you have a lovely place here, and I ask for
shelter for a few days."

"I can give you that," she replied, with a laugh.

I have said that Madame Faubourg was pretty and bewitching, but how poorly those words describe her appearance. She was more than pretty and bewitching. She
was superb. Her figure was luxuriously rounded, her eyes
coal black and fringed with long eyelashes, and her cheeks
as rosy as those of a child.

I was given a delightful room, airy, comfortable and
handsomely furnished. After supper I retired to my
apartment and removed my coat and vest and encased my
feet in slippers, and with a cigar prepared to make myself
at rest with the world. I lolled back in a huge, easy
chair, and placed my feet on a marble-top table. And as
the smoke went in clouds towards the ceiling I thought of
Madame Faubourg, her eyes and her figure. And so I
thought and thought until my head commenced nodding
on my breast.

"Monsieur!"

My eyes opened like a flash. The very object of my thoughts was standing before me, and—but, pshaw! I have suppressed her name—she was en dishabille. Her white, full bosom was partly exposed, and there was a careless abandon in her dress that sent the blood through my veins like fire. I arose to my feet hastily, and cried as I approached her:

"Madame Faubourg, what am I to understand?"

"Hush!" she cried, with her fingers to her lips. "Say not a word but follow me."

The shadows of night had already fallen, and as she led the way into the hall she looked quite spectral in her white attire. I uttered not a word but followed her steps mute and silent. What could she mean? I felt as if I was breathing the air of a furnace.

Near the end of the hall she turned and entered a room where I mechanically followed her. A lamp on the dressing-case was burning dimly, but by its light I was enabled to see that the apartment was furnished with considerable extravagance, yet with good taste. The atmosphere was sensual with the odors of flowers and cologne.

When we had once entered the room Madame Faubourg suddenly stopped and gave me one long, yearning look, and I felt an irresistable desire to clasp her to me. Probably the wild, hungry look in my eyes led the woman to divine my thoughts, for she hastily passed me and closed her chamber door. Then she turned the key in the lock and transferred the key to her bosom.

Again our eyes met.

Unconsciously my arms opened to her while my head whirled in a maze. I did not see her approach, but suddenly felt her arms around me, and her hot lips crushing against mine. I could not breathe! I could not see! A convulsive tremor traversed my frame and I sank exhausted and helpless to a lounge with the woman in my arms. I awoke to my senses again, however, by her sudden withdrawal from my embrace. I sprang after her but she evaded me and cried in a determined voice:

"Stop!"

I stood still while a low, mocking laugh escaped her lips.

"Do you think I am a fool?" she suddenly cried in a low, sneering tone.

I was bewildered and did not know what to say. I could only gasp out "Madame," and then stare blankly at the woman. Madame Faubourg had me subjected and she knew it. She stepped up close to me and cried in a subdued, threatening voice:

"I would like to ask you one question, sir, and that is, what are you doing in my room?"

What was I doing in your room? The words aroused me to action. I saw again the woman enter my apartment and beckon me to go with her. A feeling of anger and defiance passed over me, and I replied calmly:

"Because you asked me to go with you."

"Do you not know," continued Madame Faubourg regardless of my answer, "that I am a married woman? You do not? Well, I am. I was married this morning and my husband at this moment is down stairs."

"Are you trying to blackmail me?" I demanded fiercely.

"Monsieur; I am sorry but I need $100 and you must give me that amount."

"And if I don't?" I said, coldly.

She leaned toward me and cried:

"I shall scream until my cries arouse the house, and my husband, the boarders and the neighbors will rush to my assistance. I tell you, Monsieur, the laws of Michigan are very strict with ruffians who endeavor to ravish reputable women."

"Ravish reputable women?" I gasped.

"Yes, she cried, meaningly."

Then I saw how completely I was in her power. I pressed my temples with my hands and took several hasty strides across the floor.

"Now don't be foolish," said Madame Faubourg. "You had better pay the money and save yourself trouble."

"You have played your game cleverly," I said, "but I will get even with you yet. My money is in my coat pocket and if you will go to my room I will give you $100. You see my coat and vest are in the room."

"I cannot," said the woman. "Once I leave this room you are out of my power."

I drew my diamond ring from my finger and said:

"Take this for security."

"That would be nice security. People would want to know what I was doing with your ring. No, nothing but money."

Madame Faubourg astonished me with her shrewdness. She was indeed an accomplished blackmailer.

"Well, then," I said, desperately, "what am I to do?"

Madame Faubourg was very pale but marvelously calm and collected. She thought for a moment and finally said:

"Are you a man of your word?"

The words made me think of the woman who put the question, but I said:

"I am."

She crossed the room and took a small book, which I found to be a Bible, from a drawer in the bureau.

"Swear on this," she said, "that if I go to your room you will give me $100."

"I will," I answered slowly.

She repeated an oath and I followed her as she spoke.

"So help you God," cried the woman, her face growing paler every moment under intense excitement.

"So help me God," I echoed somewhat nervously.

She said no more but took the key and opened the door. We passed from the room together into my apartment. Once we had entered there I said nothing but waited for Madame Faubourg to speak. She looked into my eyes and I returned her look with a cold, deliberate stare. Her lips twisted nervously as she gasped:

"The money."

I knew it was not the act of a gentleman but I could not control myself, and without saying a word I raised my foot and kicked—kicked, great scott, I kicked the marble top table over and raised a horrid din. My eyes opened and there stood my old school mate in the doorway with a rather surprised look on his face.

"Did I frighten you, old man. I am sorry but I came to bid you good night. I guess you must have been asleep."

Asleep! asleep! I looked around.

"Here is Our Hero"

"Yes, asleep," I answered, "and dreaming!"

"You should have been down stairs; Madame Faubourg has been amusing us with some delightful operas. You know the Madame is a beautiful singer."

I am sorry, dear readers, that I am compelled to end this way, but if you are surprised one-tenth as much as I was when I awoke and found my adventure but a dream then the object in writing this story has been accomplished. Au revoir!

CHAPTER XVL.

A Modern Lawyer.

WHEN I was still in my teens parental judgment resulted in my being installed in a lawyer's office. Whether or not it was thought I would shine with any particular splendor in the midst of the brilliant galaxy of legal lights that then illuminated Detroit I am unable to say, but nevertheless the fact remains. I was given into the hands of an astute and learned desciple of Blackstone, who, it was asserted, would quickly instruct me into the requirements of his profession, and thereby place me on the high road to success and prosperity. I was meekly cognizant of the magnificent prospects which had opened so opportunely before me, and with much embarrassment and many blushes I entered on my new career. The gentleman who was to do the steering of my frail and untutored craft, was a large and portly man, of much dignity and military carriage.

He was a study in himself.

On first acquaintance, he could not help but excite the utmost admiration mingled with a certain feeling of awe; but on after inspection, the first formed opinion would necessarily be compelled to undergo a great many changes. As I looked at the gentleman in question, being particularly attracted by his physical appearance and dignified bearing, I paused for a moment in my wonderment, and began to take in his other features.

I saw his coat, cut a la Prince Albert, worn, threadbare and old fashioned. It was out of place. It was not the coat of humility worn by the miser. No; the owner

was too proud for that. What did it infer then? Poverty!
Impossible! More likely the negligee of genius!

And yet there were other things that aroused the mind
to thought. The poorly furnished office, and the legal
parchments and law books, grey in their coating of undis-
turbed dust. Was he poor after all? Would poverty
dare follow such dignified and magnificent bearing? Was
there not talent to ward off its insidious advances?

Yes; there was talent—talent simply dazzling in its
character. He was a man of remarkable learning and
brilliant attainments, with the tongue of an orator and
physique of an actor—the very embodiment of genius.
Yet in spite of all this I soon realized that this somewhat
mysterious gentleman was in decidedly straightened circumstances. In fact the first day of my appearance in
his office we had a most unwelcome caller in the person of
the landlord of the building, who in a very demonstrative
and loud manner, something I thought entirely uncalled
for, demanded rent for the office. It required the lawyer's
most persuasive eloquence to get the angry fellow into the
hallway. When he had gone he turned to me and remarked:

"A very troublesome man."

"How so?" I inquired with assumed innocence.

"He will insist upon bothering me for rent."

"And how much is due him?"

"A miserable $500. He is a most violent man, and if
he is not more polite in the future, I am afraid that I shall
be compelled to move."

He then dropped the subject, and as he strode across
the room, commented on the beautiful sunlight which
filtered through the closed blinds, using language which
filled me with much admiration.

"Young man," said he finally, halting in front of me,
you have entered upon a very noble profession, and one
"which affords a man of brains and push, every opportunity
in [the world to get ahead. Your father and I have been
life long friends, and if you possess a tithe of his ability
you cannot help but succeed."

This flattering reference to my father, brought the
warm blushes to my cheeks, and I bowed my head in
modest acknowledgement of his words.

"Ahem!" he finally continued, after the manner of a

man who broaches an unpleasant subject, "the pay of an attorney's clerk is very small."

"That makes no difference to me," I hastened to remark.

"His face grew brighter, and he smiled with considerably more affability upon me than heretofore.

"I see," said he, "that we shall get along in a magnificent manner together!"

I said nothing but blushed again. Seeing which he said:

"You have not seen very much of the world. How old are you?"

"Seventeen."

"You are remarkably well developed for your age. What you lack most is worldly experience. Have you ever read 'Old Curiosity Shop' by Charles Dickens?"

"No, sir."

"Read it, my boy. There is one character in it I particularly admire. It is an English solicitor named Brass, who is marvelously clever in the management of his legal affairs. You can get some very good points by perusing the book with care and attention."

"You have read a great deal?"

"I have. I have read everything worth reading in English literature."

The huge smile which followed these words bespoke intense self-satisfaction. He was conscious of his learning and did not allow the opportunity to go by without impressing me with his vast importance. As we were speaking the rustle of a woman's dress was heard in the hallway. The lawyer pricked up his ears, and in an instant darted out of the office. In a few minutes he returned radient with smiles.

"She was a beautiful woman with a divine form! I wonder what she wants with lawyer Snooks. Snooks aint no kind of a man for her. I noticed that she gave me a very tender glance as she passed into his office. My boy, my figure catches the women and brings me more business than you can imagine."

I agreed with him mentally though I made no remark.

"By the way," said he, "go into Snook's and inquire the time of the day and notice what they are talking about."

I passed into Snook's office. I found him in very close conversation with a flashily attired woman of about thirty. I ascertained the time and then withdrew. When I returned I was at once greeted with:

"Well, what are they speaking of?"

"I couldn't hear. They were speaking too low."

He paced up and down the room nervously, and seemed lost in thought. Now and then he would murmur:

"Damn that Snooks!"

Unable to control his feelings he wandered out into the hallway. He was not kept in suspense long, however. The woman finally emerged from Snook's office. She glanced in the direction of my employer, and the coquettish expression which stole over her face showed at once that she was no spring chicken. The roguish eyes were irresistable and the lawyer coughed slightly.

"It's a pleasant day," she said, looking shyly into his face.

He accepted the invitation to speak and in a few minutes they were in close conversation. Finally they entered his office. My employer whispered:

"Please excuse us for awhile."

We looked towards the door. I understood him. I picked up my hat and hastily took my departure.

"Come back in half an hour," he cried after me.

I returned in half an hour. The door was closed. I took the liberty of looking through the keyhole. I saw a sight which held my eyes glued to the keyhole, and the high estimation in which I had held my employer was very materially lowered. The woman did not seem in a hurry to leave and went off on another half hour's promenade on the street. When I returned for the second time she had gone. My employer was in his wonted lively spirits. He shook me by the hand and said I was a wonderful fellow and would certainly make a great name in the legal world.

"I secured that woman as a client," said he.

"Very good." I replied. "Much money in the case?"

He thought a while before he replied. Finally he said, with a sly grimace which was not intended for me:

"Yes; and she paid me in advance."

He chuckled softly and put both hands deep into his pockets. I heard no clink of money, and a remark which he made later on reminded me of his words and actions then.

"I want to give you a few instructions," he resumed. "You must first learn to observe."

I thought I had learned a great deal by observing, but he little knew what was passing in my mind.

"I want you to stand on the sidewalk a great deal of your time," he continued. "Watch the people carefully. When you see a man who is in trouble try and engage him in conversation."

"How I am to tell that he is in trouble?"

"Easily enough."

"And how?"

"He may be nervous and excited; or bear marks of violence on his face or hands, or his clothes may be torn as if he had a fight."

"Yes, sir."

"When you engage your man in conversation take occasion to refer to my legal ability and the cheapness of my rates. I think you can get me a great deal of work, and rest assured my young friend, I shall not forget you."

"Yes, sir."

"And again, take the morning papers and scan them closely and look out for libelous matter."

He then explained what might be termed "libelous matter."

"Mark the papers and then I shall know what to do. I tell you, my boy, there is a great deal of money in libel suits if they are properly conducted."

"Yes, sir."

"And any amount of free advertising," he added. "You can take anybody and they will think they have a grievance against a paper. A great deal of judgment must be exercised in picking out your clients. Now remember that, for that is a strong point."

He lapsed into silence for a few minutes, at length he said:

"Confound it! I have got to pay that washerwoman to-day and I haven't a dollar in my pocket."

"I thought the woman paid you in advance," I mildly remarked.

"So she did—bub—bub—"

He blushed and stammered in confusion, while I

looked as demure and blandlike as a child. At length he snatched his hat and hastily left the office saying: "You can close up about 4 o'clock I shall not be back."

I read law with this remarkable gentleman about six months. At the expiration of that time I concluded that I had had enough of law and turned my attention to other business. But this man was often the subject of my thoughts.

Why was he unsuccessful in his business?

This was a question that I frequently asked myself. One day I listened to him trying a case. It was then that I realized why his learning and ability stood him in such little part.

Egotism was what ailed him.

During the progress of the trial he seemed to forget his client entirely. He centered all his attention on himself. His antics amused the audience but angered the judge. And when the jury brought in the verdict of guilty I was not in the least surprised.

His egotism increased.

I saw him again in a law suit. His actions then proclaimed a weak mind. A few days afterwards he was taken to the Pontiac insane asylum hopelessly insane.

Egotism had killed him.

CHAPTER XVII.

A Memory of the Past.

IN a graveyard in winter time. It was late in the afternoon and the day was becoming mantled with the leaden hue of twilight. The air was filled with light particles of snow which were quickly covering the ground and surroundings with its fleecy white flakes. It was indeed a scene of deathlike stillness, without a sound stirring, save the low rustling of the wind now and then through the leafless trees and the abrupt corners and points of the little chapel in the vicinity. The chapel was old and fast falling under the cruel ravages of rust and decay. The style of architecture was decidedly antique, and the gables and turrets were made all the more indistinct and jumbled together by thick, climbing ivy and the white snow. The ivy seemed to cling to the chapel with an affectionate fondness and care as if to shield it from the cold, wind and snow. A short distance away stood a modest marble stone, which was inclined slightly forward and I saw that any rude jar would quickly precipitate it on the grave. It was a poor and wretched memento of the dead, and the grave and stone had evidently been neglected a great many years. And though the place would be passed by with heedless disregard by hundreds, to me it awakened the bitterest of memories. When I took my handkerchief from my eyes, through the fast falling tears, I saw the one word—

JOSEPHINE.

"I wish that I were dead!" Dead! Years had passed

and yet I had never forgotten those words. And I suppose that I shall never forget them either. And, standing
before that grave, with what cruel force the sentence came
to me again.

As I stood there alone, sad and thoughtful, with the
tears slowly trickling to the ground, my thoughts began to
slowly pierce the veil of the past. And a beautiful girl
face slowly assumed form, as the outlines of a
statue are brought to view by the gradual removal of the
shroud that protects it. Many years had passed, but the
beauty of the countenance still remained in my memory.
The face was oval-shaped and the finely moulded brow was
almost hidden beneath clustering curls of a beautiful
golden shade. The eyes were large, dark and fringed with
long, black eyelashes, while the rounded cheeks were
tinged with a delicate pinkish hue. At first, however,
when I aroused this picture from the past, there was an
impassiveness about the countenance which chilled me.
But it was only for the moment. The face soon awoke into animate life, but looked so sad; oh, so sad! It was a face
as pure and as innocent and as free from guile as I would
imagine that of an angel to be. She was my little sweet-
heart and we were engaged to be married. That she loved
me I could not doubt, and that I loved her was most manifest. It seemed but yesterday that I held my little darling girl in my arms and was breathing words of love in
her ears. But then I was young and age had not enfeebled or made my body rheumatic. But now my silver-
ed beard and the ills that flesh is heir to, were a cruel,
bitter confirmation that years, aye, and many of them, too,
had passed since those days of love and sweet romance.
Gone, never to come again. Gone! Gone! I could have
thrown my wretched body on the grave and ended my ex-
istence then and there.

Time—cruel Time! Onward it goes! Never stopping;
never hesitating! Only Onward! Onward! Onward!
Sweeping along with irresistable force, a force that seem-
ingly increases in velocity, but it only seems. The great
awful current called Time never changes. It is always the
same, rolling along into the futurity like a huge roaring
river endeavoring to find its level. But the level of Time

is in Heaven and when earth shall cease to be no more. Whatsoever it touches there will its awful imprint be found. The evidence of its presence is seen in the crumbling towers, walls and citadels on every hand, and even in the poor harmless flowers, that now hang withered and colorless, that so soon before were gaily blushing in radiant hues and fairly sparkling in the bright voluptuousness of life; and finally in Man himself, the noblest and grandest work of God. To-day he is in the full pride of his mental and physical vigor and to-morrow his tottering figure and poor weak mind show that the Shadow of Death, the awful advance guard of Time, has already marked its victim.

———

As the roses fade and die so fled the color from my Josephine's cheeks. She drooped and withered like the delicate flower that she was until she lay helpless in an invalid's bed. It is the good that die and the bad that live. Those words are cruel, bordering on blasphemy probably, but then they are apparently realized so often that the shadow of truth is almost given to the assertion. I held my little girl's thin, wan hand, and knelt down near her cot in silent prayer vainly endeavoring to stay my emotion. I knew that she was awaiting for me to speak but I could not give utterance to my thoughts, I brushed back the curly, disheveled hair from her pale, white brow almost unconsciously, and then sobbed as if my heart would break while our tears flowed unremittingly. After a lapse of several minutes our grief became exhausted. We were happy, however, in being alone together. Finally, my darling Josephine pushed me gently away while she pressed her hands over her eyes. Her sobs and tears broke out anew, while I, the poor wretched devil that I was, could only weep in sympathy. Finally she spoke. I saw it was with an effort and some pain. The words were uttered slowly and with an emphasis that nearly killed me. Looking at me steadily, she said,—"I wish that I were d—" I put my fingers on her lips, and cried,—"My God! Don't say that!" An unusual light came into the beautiful eyes, while she seemed to look beyond—beyond into

———"that bourn from
Whence no traveler returns."

Slowly the words came again,—"I wish that I were dead!"

"Drunk!" A man had touched me on the shoulder, and when I turned I saw I was in the grasp of a policeman. "You are drunk," he snarled. "What are you doing?" "This is the grave of my Josephine," I growled. "Look again," he snapped. I looked and saw that I had misread the name on the stone. It was

JEMIMA.

In spite of my violent opposition, and finally my tearful protestations, I was carted away in the patrol wagon and remained over night in the station.

CHAPTER XVIII.

How Does this Catch You?

I HAVE heard of crimes, black—black ones, too, whose dark shadows steal to Heaven for the light Divine interference. Crimes that even now—in imagination, my very soul revolts at their recollection and a shudder traverses my frame. Often—often have I cried in appeal, with pale, upturned face, and with all the anguish of a mind surcharged with grief and horror—"Heaven! can such things be?"

I recoil, helpless and prostrated, with tear-bedimmed cheeks and bowed head, as I read the living answer on every hand. Aye, it is only too true—too true! I crush my hands to my eyes in a vain endeavor to shout out the monster Crime, bathing in its element of tears, while in the dark, storm-cast scene is heard the groans and sighs of the weak, downtrodden and suffering.

She stole into my heart on the bright sunbeam of love and warmed my thoughts into ecstasies of delight and pleasure, and ere long the glorious perfume of orange blossoms pervaded our path, while the bells rang out their gleeful notes in the warm midsummer air. We were married. It needed not the blushing cheeks of my bride to tell this—Nature! sweet Nature herself, with her radiant and beautiful flowers and carolling birds seemed to tell the holy tale. We loved! Never could there have been such love as ours! A ray of love from the shining throne of Heaven, must have pierced and cemented our hearts together in the tender bonds of affection. And from the Fairyland of romance and idealism we plucked our home —a cottage almost hidden 'neath the foliage of creeping vines and sweet-scented flowers.

What joy—what bliss was ours! Weeks—months flew by and naught interrupted the current of our mutual love and affection. It was a dream—a living dream, in which we revelled in a mad waste of pleasure.

The crisis came! The awful black cloud of trouble entered the portals of our most peaceful home and shut out the lights and stilled our mirth and laughter. The face of that visitor I shall never, never forget! I shall never forget it, because it robbed me of my more than life—the love of my darling wife! With the help of Providence I may forgive, but I cannot—I can never forget!

That face! I see it now. The cold, cruel smile; the wicked flash of the eye, and the hard lines about the mouth. No love, no mercy there! The lineaments of those features only spoke of selfish advancement and insatiable greed—they bore the indelible stamp of the spirit that lived within. The roses of our happiness were brutally strewn at our feet, while the ruthless destroyer stamped them into an irrevocable mass. Down—down I went into this hell of misery; and in my last dying efforts, with only my fingers clinched on the edge, I saw that face, perfectly horrid in its gloating and exulting light, peering into mine!

That face—that face! And as a broom struck me over the head and brought me back to life again, I recognized —my mother in-law.

CHAPTER XIX.

The Matinee Masher.

THE matinee masher.

He is a strange and interesting character and of extremely ornate and curious construction.

He is peculiarly an American institution and thrives exclusively in large and populous cities.

He walks with a mincing gait and carries his arms akimbo, while his little brow is made all the more insignificant by long and wavy bangs.

His ties are startling in their variety of colors, and his collars would undoubtedly conceal his head were it not for the remarkable size of his ears.

Poor fellow!

And yet he is happy!

He floods himself with eau de cologne and prides himself on the length of his immaculate cuffs and the little handkerchief which protrudes from his outside coat pocket.

He speaks with a drawl. His eyes are languid in appearance and his movements decidedly blase.

He belongs to a club and frequently refers to it in conversation. He smokes cigarettes and now and then endulges in a little seltzer and wine.

He abominates beer declaring it a low and vulgar beverage.

He chums with "Cholly and "'Arry" and says "deuced" and "awfully clevah." He relates with gusto his alleged numerous amours and escapades with actresses.

All the girls dote on him.

And why?

Pshaw! he cawnt tell don't cherknow!

During the performance he promenades the floor back of the' seats in the parquette circle deeply absorbed in sucking his cane.

Now and then he says to his compatriot, 'Arry:

"What a beastily show don't cherknow."

But 'Arry has his mind turned elsewhere.

"Do you know, chummy" saps 'Arry, "that Augustus has been sadly indisposed of late."

"No; you don't tell me?"

"But I assure you, deah fellow!"

"Well, well!"

"Ah, yes!"

"And what ails the poor boy?"

"Poisoning!"

"You astonish me! Suicide?"

"Naw!"

"Naw?"

"Naw!"

"And what then?"

"Cawnt you guess?"

"Don't say guess. Its so bloody American."

"Well, cawn't you tell?"

"Naw!"

"Naw?"

"Naw!"

"Well, chummy, I learned the secret after a desperate research."

"So?"

"So!"

"What then?"

"You will remember the new cane that he purchased lately."

"I cawnt remember."

"You cawnt?"

"Naw!"

"Naw?"

"Naw!"

"Well, he did purchase a new cane lately."

"So?"

"So."

"And what's that got to do with the poisoning?"

"Everything."

"Everything?"

"Everything."

"Well."

"The cane had a big gold head.   That's the joke."

"What's the joke?"

"The gold head."

"What are you driving at, deah fellow?"

"Nawthing."

"Nawthing?"

"Nawthing."

"Well."

"The gold head—te-hee!—was brass!"

"Brass?"

"Brass.   The foolish fellow put it in his mouth and came near dying of blood poisoning."

"Great Gawd!"

"Fact."

"Fact?"

"Fact."

"Gay" But Sinful

CHAPTER XX.

One Ruined Life.

A STRANGE story, yet true, and permeated with all the attractive features of a romance. It was told to me amid a cloud of smoke as we sat together in a room in a hotel. We were both looking on a large portrait of a woman, which was placed against the wall at the foot of the bed. The picture was encased in a large and heavy frame. It was that of a woman of twenty-five or twenty-six with a bright and intelligent face, large dark eyes and a general expression of pleasing refineness about her features.

"This is the picture of a woman," said my companion, "who literally holds my life in her hands. That face I think more of than anything else in this world. No one knows what I have suffered since my acquaintance with that woman but He that knows all things.

"My friend, I have been drawn towards you by some irresistable force. We meet some people and they repulse us; with others, however, a friendship is consummated on first appearance. I like you and you have my confidence. To prove it I give you my brief story.

"A proud, aristocratic, mercenary woman, who had been separated from her husband by death; her daughter almost a child, innocent and pure; myself, a proud, ambitious young man attending college and preparing for the clergy; the man accustomed to the world, rich, cold-hearted, a gambler, dissipated and addicted to the use of opium.

"These are the characters in my story. I loved the woman's daughter and this tender feeling was returned.

We became engaged and patiently awaited my ordination
as a minister when we would be united in the holy bonds
of matrimony.

"The proud mother interfered.

"She looked with favor on the man of wealth, notwithstanding the black and foul stain on his name. He asked
for her daughter's hand in marriage and she told him yes.

"Need I tell you what followed?

"My arms were extended in vain towards the woman I
loved. The heartless mother's will prevailed. She tore
her daughter from me and forced her into the other's arms.
They were married.

"Gold filled the void where love should have been.

"Then our lives became a chaos of misery and shame.
I abandoned my sacred studies and resorted to liquor and
evil associates to kill the memory of the past. My name
became linked in a terrible scandal. I was arrested and
thrown into prison.

"After a long trial I was acquitted, but my name was
held in odium by all who knew me. In the meantime the
woman I loved was living in the keenest misery.

"Her husband treated her with indifference, and
gave himself up to drink and opium. Finally, while be-
reft of his senses with delirium tremens, he took his life.
This was shortly before my arrest. When I came out of
jail I was a free man, but did not dare to look my darling
Annie in the face.. I fled from the city to the west.

"I had a portrait of Annie and I took it with me.
That is the picture, and I never separated from it although
I have been all over the western country and even through
Mexico. At times I have been without money or friends.
I sold everything but that picture to keep me alive. I
have returned to the city from where I fled two years ago
in disgrace.

"But look at me!

"See what a wreck I have got to be! 'I live without
aim in life, devoid of ambition, friendless, moneyless, and
helpless!"

The unfortunate man burst into a flood of tears, and
for some time was unable to control his feelings.

He fled from the room before I could detain him.

In two hours he returned.

He presented a terrible appearance.

His hair was disheveled, his eyes red and wandering, and his walk unsteady.

He was drunk!

I helped him into bed. "My friend," he grasped. "Raise the picture up so I can see it better."

I did as requested.

"Don't leave me," he added. "I feel as if I were going to die to-night. Quick! quick! Put your hand on my heart. Is it beating? It don't feel so!

"My friend, if I die to-night don't fail to tell my darling mother that my last thoughts were of her.

"And Annie! God bless her! Tell her I thought of her also.

"Oh, Annie, you little know what trouble you have caused in this world."

His eyes rested in silent devotion on the picture until they closed in the stupor of a drunken sleep.

Two days later the poor devil lowered his valise and picture out of the hotel window into the alleyway below.

He then left the hotel as quietly as possibly to escape his paltry board bill.

Where he went to I know not.

I have not heard of him since.

Probably he is dead.

Who cares?

It is such memories as this that sends the chill of despair to the heart, and one realizes that there is something else besides sunshine and castles in this life.

CHAPTER XXI

"Guilty, Your Honor!"

 DELICATE child, of fragile appearance, with the stamp of innocence and purity on her sweet young face, of retiring and shy disposition make the hallowed picture of an angel from Heaven.

The imprint of innocense on a woman's face should be the pale of protection to her honor and character.

And yet there are brutes in human form who never hesitate in putting the first shameful blush to a maiden's cheeks.

The picture of a cold, heartless man winning the confidence of a mere child, and by gaining her good opinion takes upon himself the privilege of breathing words of passion into her ears, is a terrible one indeed.

Soon the cheek grows callous to the blush, and words often repeated lose their full import and meaning.

The unwilling arms grow resistless in the warm embrace of the other.

Then comes the telling crisis in her life.

Her fall marks the beginning of a descent with terrible rapidity, through all the grades of vice, sin and shame, until one day she totters into the gutter, ragged and dirty, friendless and uncared for, the object of wicked jest and rude mirth.

"I am guilty, your honor!"

Guilty of what? Guilty of drunkenness and raising a disturbance on the streets.

A young woman, in elegant but not refined attire, of beautiful features, but somewhat marred by an over abundance of powder and paint, stood in the Police Court.

Notwithstanding the change in her appearance, I recognized the prisoner as the once charming bell of an interior Michigan village.

She ran away from home with an unfeeling scoundrel and came to Detroit.

There was no marriage.

In vain she pleaded that she be made a wife before she become a mother.

She became neither.

The rascal was old and experienced in crime.

A physician, an unscrupulous man and a disgrace to an honorable profession, was called in.

When he had committed his unnatural crime the young woman was turned into the street.

She sought employment without avail and was finally compelled to resort to almost anything to prevent starvation.

Such is often the case of a life of shame.

It is not only the weak that fall but the strong as well.

The young woman was soon lifted into all the splendor of the early stages of dissipation.

She dressed in silks and sparkled in diamonds.

She accepted her new life with avidity and plunged headlong into a wild and dissolute career.

Finally she brought up in court, and with the indifference begotten of evil association, acknowledged that she was guilty of drunkenness.

"My daughter! Oh, my daughter! And has it come to this?"

An old, grey haired man, enfeebled with age and intense mental suffering staggered out into the middle of the court room.

The tears were flowing down his pale and wrinkled face and his trembling hands were extended towards the beautiful woman at the bar.

A slight tremor was noticeable about her lips.

Then a hard, cold look stole over her features.

The pretty head was thrown back and she cried to the judge in two, indifferent, metallic words:

"The fine?"

"Ten dollars or sixty days in the workhouse!" came the answer.

The money was paid at once and the woman swept from

the court room just as her aged father staggered forward and fell insensible to the floor.

The human heart is indeed strangely constructed.

Its feelings are as diverse as the veins that spread over the body.

Stranger scenes are being daily enacted in life that can ever be found in romance.

People grow hardened and unnatural by continually living in an atmosphere of vice and crime, and look with indifference on scenes that melt others into tears.

Such was the case of this young woman, whose nature had become so warped that she knew not even filial love, affection or sympathy.

* * *

"My darling!"

An old grey-haired man attired in the dress of a person of wealth, was clasping the woman, who but a few hours before was in the Police Court, in his arms.

They were alone and in a luxuriously furnished apartment.

"I want you for my wife," continued the old man. "I care not what the world may say. My wealth will silence all talk and disgrace."

The little woman looked down modestly towards the floor.

Then coyly raising her eyes, she cried:

"Old stuff! give me your flipper! I am yours every time, and you can gamble on that and win, you bet!"

CHAPTER XXII.

The Chronic Juror.

NOSE bulging luminous and resplendant; a countenance unshorn and begrimed with dirt; eyes small, red and bleary; a gait, weak, shambling and uncertain, with a figure attired in thread-bare apparel, and a hat slouched low down on the forehead may suggest the appearance of the hero of this chapter.

The chronic juror.

And where are his haunts?

The police and justice courts and in the offices of the coroners.

Now and then he wanders into the higher courts. But the quarters are strange to him and he is content to hide away in the last row of seats.

But in the Police Court it is different. In that judiciary he feels perfectly at home. He assumes an abandon of behavior quite charming.

In the justice courts he is still more at ease. He throws his legs on the back of the benches, and quaffs the air, if it were so much nectar.

But in the companionship of the Coroners he revels in a sort of luxury difficult to describe. He feels at home and converses with great familiarity with all who may come in contact with him, and yet at the same time he assumes a graveness of demeanor only equalled by the sepulchral bearing of the owl.

And, by the way, I have known Coroners who have greatly cherished the chronic juror.

And why?

Well, for financial reasons.

Financial reasons? Money to be made out of these wretched, bedraggled specimens of humanity.

Yes.

And how?

Various ways.

I have known Coroners, each one of whom, made it a practice of keeping three or four chronics at his beck and call.

An inquest brings a juryman $1.50 and sometimes more.

The Coroner in consequence of favoritism demands his little "divy."

And then the chronics are also compelled to do the Coroners dirty work.

They are called upon to straighten out the "stiffs" and get them in something like shape for their master's inspection.

And what can the chronics make a week?

A great deal depends on the time of the year.

Now in the spring time, when the winter's ice is breaking up, numerous "stiffs" are fished out of the river, and accordingly the inquests are not few in number.

One of the great features of the chronic is his verdict.

Like all good business men he has got that well regulated.

Or the Coroner has got it well regulated for him.

It makes little difference.

It is a verdict all the same.

His cases of "accidental drowning" and "suicide while temporarily deranged" are as numerous as the flowers or the "stiffs" that bloom in the spring tra-la!

The way that the chronic arrives at his verdict makes an interesting study.

And how is it accomplished?

First the testimony is heard, which, from long experience, the chronic does not allow his mind to be burdened. with.

After that comes the retirement and deliberation.

To give the deliberation all the play necessary he pulls out his short, black clay pipe and takes a puff or two of tobacco.

After a few minutes the chronics look at one another and nod their heads.

"What a Beautiful Woman."

The verdict has been arrived at.

The foreman, he of the prodigious snout, fills out the blank paper passed in by the Coroner.

It's another case of "suicide while temporarily deranged."

And when they file into the awful presence of the Coroner again they bow in owl-like silence, significant of their full approval when the foreman tells the result of their deliberations.

It is a wonder this foreman don't make a mistake and write "accidental drowning" instead of "suicide while temporarily deranged." But probably he does sometimes and it is never discovered.

Now and then the Coroner and his retinue of chronics have queer experiences. I will relate one circumstance which possesses some remarkable features bordering indeed upon the romantic.

Unrequited love caused a certain youth, whose name I cannot recall, to desert his home in Toronto, Ont. He came to Detroit. He looked for work but in vain, and seeing naught but misery and poverty in store for him, decided to bring his life to an end.

He became imbued with the idea of committing what our reportorial friends call "a rash act."

He had a few dollars left and forthwith purchased a revolver.

A few hours later he was standing on Fort street near Griswold.

He placed the revolver to his temple and fired.

The bullet crushed into the skull and the unfortunate youth sank in a heap on the stone sidewalk.

It was midday and of course the streets were crowded.

A large number of people quickly gathered around the figure of the young man.

He was quivering in the last throes of life.

He lay on his back, and the pale upturned countenance, with the classic features and the clustering curls on the broad white brow, was suggestive of a noble and manly beauty.

But he was dying.

Life, with all its sorrows and disappointments, was closing fast, and the heartless, Canadian coquette would soon be relieved of one of her many unfortunate lovers.

Fortunate woman!

Poor, deluded man!

The blood from the small, round hole in the right
temple poured out in a torrent, ensanguining the walk,
and causing an involuntary shudder to pass through those
who looked upon the dread scene.

A professional gentleman stepped forward. He stoop-
ed down and felt of the recumbent man's wrist.

At the same moment the latter's limbs stiffened and
his countenance became fixed in the awful expression of
death.

"He is dead?"

The gentleman dropped the hand and then disappeared
from view.

He was a physician and had been drawn there through
curiosity.

The Coroner arrived, and—I, the writer, blush for
shame of such a Coroner—and with him came six full-
fledged, red-nosed chronics.

They were smiling and smirking, and they nudged
and blinked at one another like so many lunatics.

They were happy.

Beer had already crimsoned the horizon of their
hopes.

They thought not of the dead; of a mother's tears and
a father's sorrow, but only of themselves.

And beer.

But it takes such men to make chronics.

"Gentlemen!"

It was the voice of the Coroner.

He was addressing his colleagues.

He had removed his hat.

Six other heads became uncovered.

"Be sworn!"

And so the jury was impanneled.

"We will adjourn to the undertakers."

They adjourned to the undertakers.

The body was conveyed there.

It was stretched out on a board.

The Coroner decided to take a little testimony prior to
another adjournment.

These adjournments are a great boon for the chronic.

Each adjournment brings in seventy-five cents extra.

No wonder there are so many adjournments in an inquest.

It pays.

Just as the Coroner was preparing himself for his important duties, great Scott! the corpse sat bolt upright, glanced around and cast off a lot of blood from its stomach.

"Why the man's alive!"

I shall never forget the look which passed over the faces of the Coroner and his satellites.

It bespoke the utmost astonishment mingled with no little chagrin.

Yes, the man was alive, and each moment he grew stronger.

He was removed to the hospital.

When he was gone the Coroner was surrounded by a crowd of anxious chronics.

"Our money!" they gasped in a chorus.

The Coroner turned on them in a huff.

He too was disgusted as well as disappointed.

"Can't hold an inquest on a live man!" he growled.

One bleary eye was turned up in the most pitiful manner, and the red sniffing nostrils told of intense mental anguish.

"But he may die?" came words in sad interrogation.

But the Coroner made no reply.

He strode angerly away.

And the six chronics held the most mournful consultation of their lives.

And now for the finish.

A love story could never be more awfully romantic than this.

For two long months a beautiful girl kneeled at the couch of the young man who had attempted suicide.

She prayed as never a woman prayed before.

And not in vain.

The young man lived.

And to-day he is happily married, and to the woman too, who caused his near approach to death.

CHAPTER XXIII.

The Abortionist.

IDNIGHT!

A cold, bleak November night.

The black, ominous skies tell of an approaching snow storm, which is also manifesting itself in light flying particles of snow.

The streets in the great metropolis of Michigan are ghost-like in their lonely and deserted appearance.

The wind is blowing with a savage earnestness, causing the belated pedestrian to bend his head and hold his feet with an effort.

Louder and louder blows the wind, while the cold, fierce air pierces the flesh, chilling the very marrow of the bones.

A sigh, a hiss, a moan, a shriek, a roar—it is the wind, like so many demons, singing in mad, wild revelry their paeans of triumph on taking possession of the city.

It was the night when a foul and awful murder became effaced from the scrutiny of human eyes and the very lips of nature were sealed—sealed by the shroud of night and the rushing, ice-cold waters of the Detroit River.

Splash!

It was a plain wooden box.

Into the water it went, disappearing at once beneath the surface, as if heavily freighted with lead.

"Gone!"

In spite of the intense darkness two deathly, white faces were seen on the edge of the river, peering at the spot where the box had sunk.

"Gone!"

In what a fear stricken tone the word was uttered.

The other replied:

"Yes, thank God!"

Thank God!

A terrible expression!

Thanking God that the awful crime of the seducer—the abortionist—the murderer had been forever obliterated!

These guilty wretches, trembling and quaking with fear, had not then the courage to grasp each others hands in a compact of future silence, but quickly hastened into their vehicle and drove away like mad from the terrible place.

They disappeared into the darkness.

Days, weeks and months rolled by.

With the warm gusts of early spring the ice in the river began to melt like frost on the window-pane when breathed upon.

And as the weather become warmer the ice broke into floes, rushing along in the current with a low, grinding noise.

The bottom of the river became stirred up, making the water yellow and muddy in hue.

One day a terrible discovery was made.

In a box, lying near the bank of the river, was found the body of a woman, horribly mutilated, and with the arms and legs tied in such a fashion, that the remains were in a heap.

An investigation followed. The body could not be identified.

But the story of a terrible crime was revealed.

That shapeless, hideous mass of bones and flesh once represented a woman, young in years, but whose beauty now could be only told in imagination.

It was evidently the same old, old story, which comes to us now on a river of tears from years long gone by, of a woman weak and foolish and a man base and designing.

She fell—fell as many a poor unfortunate had before her, while the heartless scoundrel who had wraught her ruin, not satisfied with blasting her reputation forever, must needs hasten the wretched, unoffending body into the grave.

The scapel and the drugs of the abortionist did the deed!

Abortion!

Can there be a more terrible crime against the laws of God and man than that?

A crime, the details of which, are too awful to put in print.

And yet, notwithstanding this fair city's boasted culture, wealth, and police protection, these monsters incarnate are found as easily as the gold, which buys them, clinks in the palm of the hand.

We know them!

The whispered proof of their guilt follows them wherever they go, but in consequence of their cunning and shrewdness, they generally escape the web of the law, although they may become entangled in its meshes now and then.

It is difficult to convict the abortionist.

THE END.

www.ingramcontent.com/pod-product-compliance
Lightning Source LLC
Chambersburg PA
CBHW020807020726
47495CB00008B/2625